"Love is the only force ca[...]
enemy into [...]
Martin Luther King, Jr.

"The greatness of humanity is not in being human, but in being humane."
Mahatma Gandhi

SiBoRE™ - A Simple Book Readers Edit

When you read the story, you will come across red words that may be near a red QR code cube. By using a QR code reader, you will be sent to related Internet sites. These sites are **DYNAMIC** and can be changed by the reader. This makes every reader of this book a potential editor!

Here's an example of how it works:

1. Using a cell phone camera, click on a QR code box on a page.
2. You are taken to an Internet site explaining content.
3. You have a better Internet site to explain content.
4. You then send that site link to art@myeblox.com.
5. Your site is accepted and you accept the editing agreement.
6. E-Blox Inc. changes QR code bounce to your site.
7. All future clicks on that QR code will go to your new site.
8. All future clicking on black QR99 code here will show your name and date as a dynamic editor for that QR Code. Past names, dates, and sites of editors will also be shown. There are no costs or charges for this service.

Dynamic Editors ——

qr99.myeblox.com

ISBN 978-1-09833-303-0

i

Table of Contents

How to Use QR (Quick Response) codes

To use QR codes, you must have a device with a camera that can connect to the Internet. Most cell phone cameras have this feature. Otherwise there are many free QR code readers on the Internet for all the popular handheld devices. Test QR code reader here. "OK Code Reader Working" should appear on your screen. Reading QR codes is not necessary to the plot or flow of the story and is only provided to show how fiction and reality are related.

Author's Notes

In the book *The Great Awakening*, you will find references to a worldwide pandemic. I started writing this story months before coronavirus (COVID-19) was in the news. It was almost as if the earth was speaking to me. *The Great Awakening* is actually the sequel to the book *Earth Won*. The first story was a collection of short stories written for products sold by E-Blox Inc. Each chapter was actually a story included in a product that offered hands-on building of objects in that story. The QR codes were used to give educational value to the kit of parts more than to enhance the story or plot. There were 80 QR codes dispersed in the story, and one reviewer found them very distracting. QR codes have been minimized in *The Great Awakening*. Here is a summary of *Earth Won* for those who have not read it:

In *Earth Won* there are brave people in the future with robots and pets that stand up against the evils of humanity. Seymour, his robot assistant Robyn, and his dog Glen work out of a secret laboratory and answer the mysterious calls of nature whenever their help is needed. Ruby, her robot assistant Max, and a cat named Devyn also answer mysterious calls of nature whenever their help is needed. They all meet and work together to fight an evil organization called REED and a mysterious Creature. But can two humans, two robots, two pets, and a slew of advanced technology stand up to a shadow organization and the Creature? Later a doctor named Paul with his robot Min, and his lost sweetheart Ester with her robot Feeniks help fight the war against pollution of the earth for profit.

The story *The Great Awakening* takes place a dozen years after *Earth Won*. The main characters, Seymour and Ruby, now have a son, a daughter, and twin boys. There are only 13 QR codes in the entire book and only 11 in the story itself. The reader can still change these codes if he or she has a better Internet site and become a Dynamic Editor. I also added poems that help the characters with the problems they encounter. There are three additional poems at the end of this book. The first called "Metamorphosis" describes how my love grew in the 53 years of my marriage to Maryann. She was the inspiration for everything in my life. The second and third poems are about how free will gives us the right to choose how we live. Before each poem is a comment on how that poem relates to the story. Reading these poems first may help you understand some parts of the story. There is also a QR code that will allow you to hear the characters in the story sing a children's song about love. The song is called *Skidamarink* and it was one of my wife's favorite songs to sing to the grandchildren. I hope this will help make your reading a pleasant experience. I will always appreciate feedback from readers and try to improve my limited writing skills.

I want to thank Pixabay.com for many of the royalty free images in this book.

Art Seymour

Chapter 1
Sally

The cool spring breeze softly caressed Ruby's face as she sat in Seymour's arms on the balcony of the castle. It was rare to feel a breeze inside their mountain cave, but today was different. Then a pure white crow landed on the ledge that surrounded the balcony and strutted toward them. It had been many years since Glen, the dog that answered all their questions, had gone into the light, and now they were on their own. After all the adventures the Spirit of the earth had sent to them, they both just sat still and wondered. Finally, after watching the bird bob his head up and down with an annoyed jerking motion, Ruby said "Now what?" After a moment of silence, Seymour said, "There's something in his beak." Ruby put out her hand and said, "OK, Al, drop it in my hand." Seymour gave a strange look to Ruby and remarked, "Al? You know this bird?" Ruby replied, "No. But he is obviously an albino crow so..." Seymour cut in, "Maybe our friend here is not a 'he,' but a 'she.'" After a very short pause, Ruby said, "Your right. She's too pretty to be a 'he.'" Again, Ruby extended her hand, and this time said, "OK, Sally, drop it in my hand." Instantly, the bird dropped her gift into Ruby's hand. Turning to face Seymour, Ruby smiled as if to say, "Well there you go!" Seymour laughed, took her hand gently, and said, "Let's see what your new girlfriend has brought you." Carefully picking the tiny berry out of Ruby's hand, Seymour whimsically pronounced, "It's an elderberry! I used to eat these all the time during my walks to the bayou on the Kankakee River. What do you think our feathered friend is trying to tell us?"

While they both examined the little berry, the silence was interrupted by their young daughter's voice. "Oh! I see you met Sally. Isn't she

2

pretty?" They both turned to face their daughter, Stacey, and said simultaneously, "How do you know her name is Sally?" Stacey replied, "Robyn told me when I first met Sally in the garden by the bush with all the berries on it." Robyn was a humanoid robot and guardian angel that watched over the family. She especially watched Stacey because the little girl had a tendency to explore more frequently. Robyn's metatronic brain was not only a super computer with unusual capabilities, but it also had precognition and the

ability to see things that would happen in the future. So it was no surprise to Seymour and Ruby that she knew what they would call the bird. Stacey extended her arm and Sally jumped, flapped her wings, and flew over to her like a trained pet. Ruby asked Stacey, "Where is Robyn?" Stacey replied with a young girls lack of concern, "She's helping Ester and Paul. There's some kind of an emergency." Then Stacey turned and said as she skipped from the balcony, "Come on Sally, let's go pick some flowers."

Rising from the bench, Seymour took both of Ruby's hands and pulled her close. He kissed her with a soft, lingering kiss, placed his cheek on hers and whispered into her ear, "I love you." Pulling back slowly so she could look into his blue eyes, she replied, "You better!" A small joke she used because she knew no reply was needed. They were one soul in two different bodies. Then Seymour smiled and said, "Here we go again. Let's go see what the emergency is all about."

They found Robyn helping Ester pack her suitcase. Before they could ask, Robyn without even turning to face them said, "A very contagious disease is putting people in a coma by the millions all around the world. Ester is going to REED to get groups ready to help. Paul is in the lab with Min trying to find a possible vaccine." Turning to face Seymour, Robyn looked into his eyes and said, "You have something to tell Paul?"

Seymour whispered to Ruby, "It's scary how she knows what I need to do before I do." Then taking the little berry out of his shirt pocket, pausing to look at it one more time and think about it, he finally said, "Yes, I believe I do." Then Ruby gently took Seymour's other hand and pulling him toward the door said, "Let's get moving. Sounds like some sick people need our help."

When Seymour and Ruby entered the lab, Paul, who was often called "Doc," was bent over a microscope. Min, his robotic assistant, was searching all the recorded flu vaccines on the computer screen linked to a supercomputer in another cave far away.

Without turning from her task, Min announced, "Seymour has something you should look at Paul." Ruby whispered to Seymour, "Boy, these GA's don't waste any time, do they?" Paul

4

mumbled something incoherent then glanced up at Min who had turned to look at Seymour. He jerked his head to see what she was looking at, stood up straight, and said apologetically, "Oh! Hello, I didn't hear you come into the room."

Their conversation was interrupted by the sound of childish giggles coming from a tiny, hidden speaker in a piece of jewelry hung around Ruby's neck. "The twins are up to something," Ruby said, then added, "I'll go take care of it." As Ruby turned to leave, Seymour held out his hand to Paul and showed him the small, black elderberry he received earlier from Sally, the albino crow. Paul took it with one hand, pulled his glasses out of his shirt pocket, and said, "What's this?" Before Seymour could answer, Min instructed Paul to put a drop from that berry on the comavirus under his microscope and see what happens. Paul did as she instructed because he knew that Min, like Robyn, could somehow see the future.

Paul was intensely watching as a drop of elderberry juice slowed the growth of the comavirus while Min connected the computer screen to a website that showed how elderberries were once used to combat the flu.

Seymour noticed Sally landing on a ledge of an open window high above everyone, and walking between the bars to enter the room. The bird just stood there looking down on everyone and bobbed her head up and down as if to say, "Yes, yes, yes." Then Paul, with eyes still glued to the microscope shouted, "I don't believe it!" Min added, "It's all right here on the computer display." Paul jumped like a man stung by a bee over to the display and started reading. Sally flew down, landed on Min's shoulder, and watched as Paul digested all the detailed information from the supercomputer.

Seymour was so absorbed by the excitement coming from the lab team that he never noticed Stacey. She entered the room with a vase full of elderberries, walked directly over to Paul, and waited for him to notice her. Sally finally gave out a loud crow call that sounded almost like she shouted "Paul!" Then Doc turned and, recognizing Stacey standing with a vase in her hand, he said, "Oh, hello, child. What have you brought me?" Stacey replied, "I wanted to pick some pretty flowers, but Sally would not let me. She kept pushing me over to the bush with these berries and made me pick the black ones. I tried to get some of the pretty purple ones, but Sally would yell and pull them out of my hand. She made me fill the vase with these black ones, and

then she came here. I figured she wanted me to follow her and give them to you. The flowers would have been better, but..." Paul interrupted her and said, "Sweet child, that is the most beautiful bouquet I have ever seen. In fact, right now, that is the most beautiful bouquet the world has ever seen." Then he added, "Who is Sally?"

After Paul's mind dismissed the mystifying fact that Sally was an albino crow, his thoughts returned to the emergency of the flu pandemic. He quickly and silently turned and went back to work. With the help of both Min and Seymour, they prepared many bottles of a vaccine from a diluted mixture of the black elderberry juice and distilled water. Paul tested every bottle to make sure it had the same effect on the comavirus and then labeled them and sent them to Ester. He knew that she would get REED to bring them to all the countries that were being infected.

Meanwhile, Ruby found the twins, Andy and Joey, in the playroom with Max. Max was their favorite of the GA robots, and Ruby believed it was because his voice was the same as their father's. Andy looked over at Ruby as she entered the room, and with great excitement in his voice, proclaimed, "Look mom! Joey and I made this fortune-telling machine." Then Joey added, "Max helped us a little to get it working." Ruby looked at Max who instantly proclaimed, "It's some kind of answer-maker." Ruby sat down on the floor between the twins and next to the strange-looking machine. She put her ankles under her and leaned between her knees to get a better look at the "Fortune-Telling Machine" and asked, "Can you show me how it works?" Andy said, "Just ask it a question then push that button right there on the top and you'll see."

The device was made entirely of E-Blox parts, but Ruby figured she would do what Andy said and get a few mom-like orders in at the same time. She asked, "When will Andy and Joey

7

clean up their room?" and then pushed the button on the top. Everything started to move. Lights were flashing, music was playing, a motor was turning gears, and the center tower was turning in a clockwise direction. This was not what Ruby expected so she slowly leaned back to get a better look. Then everything stopped, and a tiny little voice from the machine said, "Soon."

Andy and Joey looked at their mother, and then both started to laugh. The expression on Ruby's face was one of total surprise and shock. Seymour entered the room and, seeing the look on Ruby's face, inquired, "Now what has AJ done?" Seymour often called the twins by the one name of "A" for Andy and "J" for Joey because they always seemed to work together on everything. Ruby replied, "They made a machine that can answer any question you have. Come over here and sit down. Ask a question and push the button on the top," Joey added, "Only one question per day, so make it a good one."

Seymour maneuvered his way around Max and found a space on the floor near the structure that AJ had made. Like Ruby, he was trying to think of the best possible question that could trap the twins into doing their chores. "OK," he finally said, "Are Andy and Joey going to do what their mother wants?" He pressed the button on the top and leaned back to watch the contraption do its little song and dance, and finally stop. The tiny little voice from the machine once again said, "Soon."

This time Andy, Joey, and Ruby all looked at Seymour's face and burst out into laughter. Having expected a yes or no answer, he had the same expression of surprise Ruby displayed when he entered the room. The laughter stopped instantly when Jimmy, the oldest child, entered the room and said, "What's so funny?" Ruby asked, "You are home early, did something happen at school?" Jimmy replied, "They closed the school until further notice because of some contagious disease that is spreading all over the world. They told us all to go home and stay there until our parents were notified of what to do next. What were you all laughing at?"

Seymour stood up and reached down to help Ruby to her feet as he explained the answer machine the twins had invented. Andy told Jimmy to try it, so he walked over to the machine and said "Are many millions of people going to get sick because of this disease?" He then bent over, pushed the button, and watched the machine perform its dance and song and stop. Once again a tiny little voice said, "Soon." There was no change in the expression on Jimmy's face as he added, "That's exactly what they said at school." This time there was no laughter but instead a somber, foreboding silence filled the room. Finally, Max declared, "There is much to be done." Turning quickly, Max left the room. Everyone except the twins, followed as Max led them to the lab to join in making the medicine that Paul hoped would slow down the attack by this virus.

Max

Chapter 2
Moses

After a hard day's work in the lab making medicine, the family sat down around the dining room table to eat their supper. Robyn had prepared the family's favorite meal, corned beef

and cabbage with boiled potatoes and carrots. Seymour took one look at his plate, and instantly, his mouth began to water. He hurried everyone to sit down, bowed his head, and they all followed in silence. He then thanked God for the peace and safety the family enjoyed in these troubled times. He also thanked the earth for providing the wonderful meal. He thanked the cow for giving his life to nourish others. He thanked Robyn for making the meal. Then he thanked the children for being respectful during his prayer. Like every night, they knew that was the end of his prayer so they all quickly said, "Amen." Then with the clinking of silverware and an "Oh boy!" or two, the feast began.

After the peak pang of hunger was squashed by a few swallows of food, the conversation started. The children always waited for mom or dad to start the conversation. Finally, Ruby said, "Is anybody worried about anything they learned today?" Andy quickly responded with, "Is it true that millions of people are going to get sick from some disease?" Jimmy followed with, "They also said at school it would happen soon." Then Joey added, "Just like our answer machine!"

Sensing there was fear building in the children, Ruby swallowed a mouth full of food quickly and proclaimed, "There have been times like this before, but God loves His children and He will not let them go astray. We must all listen to His spirit here on earth and work to help the suffering people." There was a short period of silence as everyone savored the meal and contemplated Ruby's words. Finally, Jimmy changed the subject and, after a short glance at Andy and Joey, queried, "Just how did you get that contraption to say 'Soon'?" Andy replied, "Oh, that's the answer Moses the white moth gave us when we put him into a little room inside the machine. We wanted to see what he would say, so Max helped us add a very powerful amplifier with a microphone in the room that Moses lives in." Joey added, "He only talks after the lights flash and the room spins around for a while and then stops." Then Stacey butted in with, "Sometimes bugs have important things to say." Jimmy laughed and sarcastically proclaimed, "Now Stacey, that's just plain dumb!"

Ruby held up her hand, stared at Jimmy, and firmly said, "Motto time!" The whole family recited in unison, "Criticism Kills, Praise Builds." Then Ruby very gently asked, "Where did you hear that bugs talk?" and Stacey answered, "In Pappy's poem called 'The Bug and the Flea.'" Pappy was the nickname they gave for their grandfather on Seymour's side of the family, The grandfather that lived in Indiana near the Kankakee River. "I like that poem so much I memorized it." Stacey added. "Do you want to hear it?" They all answered with nods. So she stood up, pushing her chair back as she rose, took her place at the end of the table so everyone could see her, and began.

> "We can make a difference!"
> Said the bug to the flea.
> "The world will change a little
> Just because of you and me. "

"What ever could you do?
In a universe so vast,
Bugs have never done a thing
In all the years gone past. "

The tiny bug pondered his fate
As he nibbled on his leaf,
And then turning to face the flea,
He said, "It's my belief

That all of my ancestors
Were eaten by the birds
That spread the seeds, which became trees
To shade the roaming herds.

Without us bugs, there would be no shade,
And the grass would not grow.
The earth would be a barren waste.
All these things I know. "

The flea snickered, then laughed out loud,
"Why your nothing but a bug!
The way you talk the whole wide world
Should stop and give you a hug!

Well I've got to go and do my job,"
Was the last thing the flea did say.
And off he flew to find some dog
To make him scratch his day away.

The bug walked on in silence,
And as he walked, he thought
His life would make a difference.
He would not live for naught.

Even if he became a meal
For some young feathered thing,
His life would have been spent
So one more bird could sing.

She ended her recital with a bow as the whole family loudly applauded her performance. Jimmy even whistled to show his approval. Ruby thought, "Now that's more like it!" Only Seymour noticed Robyn standing quietly in the corner of the room and staring at Stacey. Robyn's eyes were sky blue, a shade he had rarely seen on her before. Curiosity made him ask, "What did you think, Robyn, of Stacey's little poem?" Robyn turned her head slowly and connected her sky blue eyes to Seymour's dark blue eyes and lovingly whispered, "I believe all the creatures on earth, no matter how small, have a mission." Then her eyes darkened, and she turned to pick up the dishes. This was not the answer Seymour expected. In fact it was not a very robotic answer at all! He knew something big was going to happen, and as Moses the moth would say, it was about to happen soon.

The remainder of the evening proceeded as usual. Robyn and Ruby cleaned the dishes and put them away. During the cleaning process, they discussed tomorrow's meals and the garden products that would need to be harvested soon. Anyone listening would have a difficult time determining the person speaking because their voices were almost identical.

The twins were doing their homework on the kitchen table and would interrupt Robyn and Ruby now and then for help. When they announced that they were done, Ruby inspected the results and pointed out a few errors they needed to correct. After passing the final inspection, they ran to the family room to play one of their favorite games called E-Moolah. They would guess different numbers on a grid and win or lose e-coins depending on the colors that were displayed. The e-coins were also used in other games played on the grid known as Scee™ DeLite.

Seymour was in the den walking on the treadmill that was built into the floor and staring at the wraparound wall screen in front of him. The screen was usually used to create the allusion of a real hike. The treadmill would tilt slightly whenever a slope or slanted path was encountered to further enhance the journey. But this time he was using the video screen as a large monitor to search the Internet. He kept briskly walking in a straight, flat path as he queried the computer to show different information.

Stacey was in her room sitting in a comfortable chair with Devyn the family cat in her lap. She had the book of poems her grandfather wrote in one hand, and was petting Devyn with the other. Trying to memorize more poems while making the cat purr lovingly brought her a feeling of peace.

Jimmy, however, had embarked on a new course of study. He was researching medicine and all the different diseases that existed in the past. Something in Pappy's poem had sparked him to make his life mean something, and since this pandemic was getting worse, he decided to investigate further. Perhaps, medicine could be the area where he could make a contribution. Being the oldest always seemed to carry with it a more intense sense of responsibility. Later, the children all had their teeth cleaned and slipped into their nightclothes. After one last family gathering for prayer, they went to their rooms and had 10 minutes before the computer slowly dimmed the lights to emulate a golden sunset.

When the lights were all out and Seymour and Ruby were laying cuddled like newlyweds in their large king size bed, Seymour proclaimed, "Did you know a white moth represents something pure, light, and soft. It represents a human soul, just as a white butterfly. A white moth can represent grace and mercy. It reminds me how beautifully simple things could be. Matter of fact, in Asian folklore, a white moth often represents the soul of a person in heaven." Then Ruby gently squeezed his hand, pulled him closer, and said, "Yes dear." Knowing this really meant "enough!" he said no more and was content at having the love of his life in his arms as he closed his eyes and let his thoughts drift him into sleep.

In the lab, Paul was still awake and talking to a holographic image of Ester at the REED headquarters. The medicine was slowing down the effect of the virus. The comavirus was mutating, however, and spreading faster than any disease she had ever seen. Ester's robot companion Feeniks had informed her that the black-hole tunnels would all be closing in 12 hours, and she needed to return soon or be trapped on the island. Paul asked how Feeniks knew when the tunnels would be closing? Ester said she assumed the GA on his plate made him a government assistant robot so the government that made him must have informed him. No one really knew where the GA's came from. All the different governments did not trust each other, and wars were ongoing between many of them. So nobody asked. Paul told her to come back before the tunnels closed and let Feeniks take care of the medicine distribution. She agreed and ended the call with, "I love you." Then the image changed to a picture of them holding hands as it slowly faded off.

After Paul retired, Max and Min remained in the lab to set everything up for tomorrow's production of medicine. Robyn stopped in to help, but to save time they telepathically told her everything was under control. They also communicated the information from Feeniks and Ester about the comavirus mutation. Even though Feeniks was thousands of miles away, he joined into their telepathic conversation. He told them to prepare for major isolation and that he would remain in the world to keep them informed. He added that the disease was man-made in a country that was looking for a chemical weapon. It got out of control and now it threatens the entire world. Knowing it was a man-made disease meant that it would be hard to cure with natural resources. They trusted the earth and the spirit that controlled everything so they closed the meeting by agreeing to wait for further instructions from the spirit.

Robyn went back to clean up the playroom before she would go into night-watch mode and contemplate the telepathic conversation she had recorded in her memory bank. The master computer turned the lights on as she entered the room, and the first thing she noticed was the answer machine sitting on the floor. She carefully picked it up and placed it on a table nearby so no one would trip on it. After picking up other scattered objects and returning them to their designated spots on the shelf, she headed for the door. Before leaving, she recalled the dinner conversation about the moth in the machine. She stopped in the doorway, turned to look at the house that Moses the moth was supposedly living in and said, "Good night, Moses." She waited for a moment but hearing no reply continued out and down the hall. The lights slowly dimmed in the playroom and silence filled the area. Everything was quiet except for a small voice that no one could hear in the playroom. It said, "Good night, Robyn."

17

Chapter 3
Lockdown

Sunrise brought with it the troubles of a changing world. A laser ball that moved from east to west at the top of the cave artificially produced the sunrise, but it still was a new day for those living there. People from the little village around the castle were gathering in the streets and demanding to know why they could not leave. The tunnels were closed. The main door that led to the valley was gone and replaced by a wall of rock and stone. During the night, many relatives from the town called Hidden Valley Village were brought into the cave and told all would be explained in the morning. Seymour's parents were the last to arrive just before the tri-blade helicopter left and sealed the large door in the roof with layers of rock and stone. Confusion was at the bare edge of chaos, when Doctor Paul with his wife Ester walked out onto a high palace balcony overlooking the town. There was no need for a microphone because the main computer was tuned in to his voice. He raised both hands high in the air and announced, "Quiet please!" His voice echoed throughout the cave, and the people all looked up as silence slowly prevailed. Paul continued, "Please watch the large screen that will soon appear on the west wall of the cave. All will be explained." Paul knew that Min had heard his request as a 50-by-50-foot holographic display started appearing on the west wall of the cave. An image of Feeniks standing in a large field with people all around him lying motionless on the ground soon came into focus. The silence was only broken by sighs of horror at what was on the display.

Next the voice of Feeniks, which was identical to Doctor Paul's voice, filled the cave. "These people are not dead. They are all in a comatose state. The comavirus now known as DP20 has infected them. DP20 was man-made

19

and designed to spread quickly. Total isolation is required to prevent infection. The coma takes only a few hours to manifest. We have taken care that you are all clean." The people knew by the robotic precision of the comments that it was Feeniks speaking and not Paul. Still, the voice made a few turn to look at Paul to see if he was the one speaking. Feeniks continued, "Man-made virus will be hard to stop. Complete isolation may be required. I will stay here and try to keep people in comatose state alive. You must find cure. Listen to Doctor Paul! I will keep you informed." The screen snapped off and for a moment dead silence filled the cave. The same voice suddenly but calmly said, "You are my family, and I want to assure you that we are going to be alright. Please, do not be afraid! I want everyone to go home and someone will come to your house with an instruction sheet to get us organized to fight this disease. Remember, the people out there are counting on us. The spirit of the world and the spirit of this community will rise to the challenge and win again." Although his voice was calm, the people could sense great confidence in his speech. They did as they were instructed, and the streets were cleared.

That day changed all of history. A new calendar was made with each day being numbered from that day forward. The first square in the calendar was labeled, LD1 for "lockdown day 1." Every day thereafter would be increased by 1 until a cure was discovered and the cave could be opened again. First, however, a daily routine to keep the people in the cave alive and healthy had to be worked out. The cave was sealed so tight that not even water could be brought in from the outside. The stream that once flowed through the cave was sealed off and dry. The enormous challenge of just living underground was the first priority.

Day 2 started with instruction sheets being given by Robyn, Max, Min, Seymour, and Ruby to every family. The first thing that was addressed was the fact that the family members brought in last night were not allowed to bring anything with them. There were people from many different ethnic groups now in the cave. A grandmother,

sitting in a chair knitting told Ruby, "I was told to take all my clothes off. The robot sprayed me down with a warm liquid she had brought and made me put on a sheet with holes for my head and arms. I could not even bring my toothbrush. Of course, I refused at first, but when she said I may never see my family again and could possibly die, I did what she asked. She said her name was Robyn. She sounded an awful lot like you." Ruby answered, "Yes, a few of the GA's have the same voices as the people they work with." Then the Grandmother asked, "GA? What's a GA?" Ruby replied, "I use to think it stood for Government Assistant, but now I believe it means Guardian Angel." The old lady looked up from her knitting and commented, "I really am thankful they let me bring my pets, I would have hated to leave them behind. The robot said they will be happy here, is that true?" Not knowing how to answer, Ruby could only say what she believed, "If Robyn told you then yes, it is true."

Each family filled out a sheet describing the skills in their household. It would take time to get

21

the cave capable of supporting those that dwelled inside. The cave was now equivalent to a space station that had to support life with no outside help. Like a space station, radio communication with the outside world was one thing that was still possible. The cave also had a very large saltwater lake in an area where the ceiling was too low for homes or gardens. Max had helped the engineers build the lake and install in the low ceiling thousands of lasers to produce strong artificial sunlight. They had diverted the little stream to fill it and then transported tons of sea salt to make the water emulate the ocean. It was then seeded with the best oxygen-producing

plankton to help make oxygen for the people living in the cave. When the oxygen was not needed, the sunlight ceiling would turn off. Now, this would be their only source of oxygen. Caretakers were quickly appointed and trained by Max to make sure this lake functioned properly.

By LD15, the town was starting to look like a well-designed corporation. Everyone knew their job and was trying their best to do what was required. Paul and Min had spent these first two weeks in the lab working on a cure and communicating with Feeniks. Ester, with Jimmy helping her, was acting as village doctor so Paul could stay focused on his work. Stacey would monitor the radio stations, but they all were gone except for the few automated transmissions that repeated the same information every day. Stacey and Sally turned to the garden and started helping the newly trained farmers. The twins and an African American boy named Martin would bring drinks to many workers during the day. Martin was a couple years older than Jimmy and new him from school. After doing their work, the twins and Martin would stop by the playroom to check on Moses. On LD15, Robyn was cleaning in the playroom when they arrived. Andy went over to the answer machine and asked, "Is anything new going to happen today?" The machine did not go through its normal dance, but instead just quickly repeated the normal "Soon." Robyn's audio sensors heard the "Soon," but her telepathic brain heard "Warn Feeniks, beware rover!" She did not know what the rover was or what the message meant but instantly transmitted the message to Feeniks. After a short delay a reply came back to her, "Thanks, you just saved me. I will explain later." The twins were complaining about the same message every day as Robyn left the room and went directly to the lab. Upon entering the room, Paul instantly said, "OK, she's here now. Tells us what is going on out there!" The holographic image of Feeniks in the middle of the group started speaking. "There are robots out here shaped like large boxes on wheels. They look a little like the Mars rover from long ago. They are selectively taking certain comatosed people to a building guarded by military robots. I tried to approach one of these rovers, and it fired a laser weapon at me. Robyn's warning came just before it fired, so I had my body shield at full power. The laser still penetrated my shield and warped my chest plate. This was a weapon-grade laser. I instantly shut down all systems and tried to appear dead. The rover inspected me then turned and went hunting through the people until it found one that satisfied its programming. A scoop came out of the front and the rover took that person to the building with the military robot guards."

Paul shouted, "Oh my God! No! No!" He slumped into a chair, put his face into his hands and started to weep. Ester went over and put her hands on his shoulders and said, "Paul, what is it?" Everyone in the room wanted to know, but they stood silently until Paul could compose himself enough to speak. He finally whimpered, "I think this could possibly be a worldwide type of genocide." Min brought him a glass of water and a clean cloth to wipe his face. After a couple swallows of water and a quick wipe of his face he continued, "I suspected this disease was man-made because of the way it was spreading. Now I think it might be the result of a worldwide organization that wants to kill everyone that does not agree with the way they think. This is something that has been well planned out for years and probably has bases in every country. I don't know what we can do to stop it." He put his head into his hands and started to weep.

Feeniks took the group's focus off Paul as he announced, "A military robot is coming my way. I think it can detect my transmission. Got to shut down," and his image blinked off. Paul looked up and sorrowfully proclaimed, "They even have a robot army ready to kill anyone or anything that tries to stop them." Every knee in the room was suddenly too weak to support standing, and everyone found a chair and sat down in silence.

Max finally broke the long silence produced by the horror, "We need to shut down all wireless communication before this new enemy locates our village. I will start the process now." Min quickly added, "I am receiving telepathy from Feeniks. He says he used his holographic shield to make him look like a large stone and the military robot inspected and moved away. Looks like he can hide, but he's not equipped to fight these military guards." Robyn added, "I will go check on the children." Ruby said, "I will go with you." Seymour quietly stood up and slowly walked out of the room.

He first went to the chapel to sit and ask all the heavenly powers to help. He did not know what to do. He remembered how Glen used to be with him in past times of trouble. A mental picture of Glen came sharply into focus as tears slowly worked their way down his cheeks on each side of his nose. Glen seemed to be saying, "Don't worry. I will always be with you to help."

Seymour used the back of his hand to wipe his face dry and left the chapel. Walking slowly through the halls of the palace, he came to the playroom. It was empty, but for some reason, he walked in and looked at the answer machine that AJ had built. He heard a soft voice say, "Use my gift." He stared at the machine in disbelief for almost a minute and heard it again. "Use my gift." Seymour left the playroom and walking faster now, he headed for the main living room. He remembered what he had read about white moths being the spirit of someone that died. "Could Moses be the spirit of Glen?" he thought. He knew what Glen had given him during the trial to fight the Creature. He was sure the Creature was responsible for making people develop this terrible virus. For the first time since Paul revealed the evil plan, Seymour felt hope. Glen had given him the power to read, understand, and control any binary language. This allowed Seymour to modify computer software with his mind. He had to use that gift to stop this catastrophe. Using Glen's gift was the answer! But how?

Chapter 4
The Gift

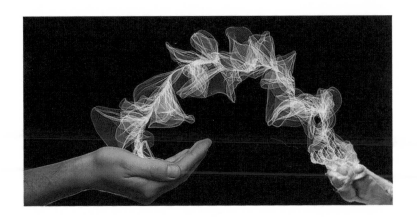

On LD22, Seymour was busy trying to use his gift from Glen to mentally change software in computers. It was easy when he was in the room with the computer, but now he had to connect from within the cave to computers in the outside world. Then late in the week, Robyn told him that Feeniks had sent her a schematic of a special hat made from a frying pan that could help connect by mental telepathy to Feeniks' metatronic brain. Everyone was on the edge of their seats when they ran the first test on the hat the next day. It worked! By holding the pan with the circuitry on his head, he was able to communicate with Feeniks just like Robyn. There were no radio waves transmitted, and he could actually see where Feeniks was scanning.

Seymour could talk to Feeniks by just thinking of what he wanted to say. Thankfully, not all of Feeniks thoughts were transmitted, just the ones he wanted to send. The same was true in the reverse direction, so Feeniks could see where Seymour was looking but only receive what Seymour wanted to say. Eager to test more, Seymour transmitted, "Get near a computer, I want to see if I can read the software!" Feeniks went over to the computer that was used to control the building he was hiding in and scanned the front panel. "I'm getting nothing. Get closer." Feeniks went over to the computer and placed his hand on the front panel. Seymour said, "Still nothing. Hold the small antenna used to transmit commands to objects in the building." About three seconds after touching the antenna, the lights in the room flashed off and on twice. "I'm in! It works!" he shouted to everyone in the room, and Feeniks also received his verbal excitement. For the first time, the group felt there was a way to fight the enemy that made this disease. But who were they?

No time was wasted on making a plan of attack. Feeniks would have to get close enough to grab the antenna on an enemy rover, and Seymour would use Glens gift to get into the software and control it. Once in control, they hoped to find out who was behind this sinister plot to put the world asleep and kill anyone that would not obey. There was one thing that worked in their favor. The coma was actually a state of suspended animation that was developed for space travel. Paul determined this human stasis from information Feeniks had sent in the beginning of the pandemic. This gave the team a little time to be cautious. They did not want to lose Feeniks. He was the only one they had in the outside world right now.

Seymour and Feeniks were working as a team now. Feeniks would search for an enemy rover while Seymour watched and advised. They found two that were too close to the military robots and decided to not take a chance with these. Then in an industrial part of the city they found one that was alone and searching factories and offices that were mostly abandoned. They decided to get ahead of the rover and hide near someone placed in an open area and sitting in a chair with his arms and head on a table. This would force the rover to approach from behind the person putting the rover camera away from the wall. After setting up the trap, Feeniks used his holographic shield and appeared to be a vending machine against the nearby wall. The perfect trap was set. Now all they could do is wait for the rover to get there.

While they waited, Seymour telepathically showed Feeniks how many years ago Glen, a Wicklow Terrier, had the power to control software in computers. He sent his memories of Glen controlling the military robots and the doors to the room that was going to be used as a courthouse. He let Feeniks see and feel the static shock that jumped from Glen's body to his chest and then the orange flow of light that went from Glens paw into his hand. After that happened, Glen no longer controlled the computers, he did. It was a gift from Glen and helped save the world from the Creature that was controlling REED. Seymour mentally added, "I believe that over the years since *Earth Won*, the Creature has infected powerful leaders all over the world to believe in the global destruction of those who will not obey him. After that, he will kill even these followers because the Creature wants this world to be only for him, his demons, and the master Satan." Feeniks only responded with, "You're right."

Suddenly, all communication ceased because the rover entered the room. It approached the person at the table as predicted. When it was focused on the person in the coma, Feeniks drop his holographic disguise, zoomed into the rover and grabbed a small antenna on top near the front panel. He predicted the rover would try to escape, so he turned on a powerful magnet that held him in place as the rover spun around and tried to buck him off. If this were an

old fashion rodeo, Feeniks would have a golden belt buckle for staying on. Then all movement stopped, and Feeniks heard, "OK. I'm in and shut it down. I'm afraid it transmitted a help code before I could stop it. I am programming it now to follow you and make no more transmissions. You better hurry. I'm afraid some of the guards are on the way to see what happened. OK, it should follow you now. Let go of the antenna and get out of there!"

Feeniks turned off his magnet and let go of the antenna. He scurried out of the building and hurried back to his hideout using untraveled roadways. The rover followed like a trained pet. Seymour took the frying-pan hat off his head and told Min to keep in touch and let him know when he's safe. Ruby could see her husband had a severe stress headache, so she offered him some pills and a glass of cold water. He said, "The water is OK, but I can't take the pills. They may affect me when we start up again. Thank you anyway." She put the pills in her pocket and stood behind him. She put her hands on his shoulders and gentle gave him a massage to help him relax. Everyone waited as Min was telepathically following Feeniks back to his hideout.

Min finally announced, "They are back in the safe place. Feeniks wants to wait for 20 minutes to make sure they were not followed." Seymour started to reach for his frying pan hat handle, but Ruby grabbed his hand and said, "Wait!" He sat back in the chair and did what she commanded like a husband that new when his wife meant what she said. His headache was starting to vanish and 20 minutes more of the massage would surely help. Precisely 20 minutes later, Min said, "OK. He's ready to resume," Seymour put on his brain hat with no resistance from Ruby as they smiled at each other. He found Feeniks was already holding the rover's antenna so he went right to work searching all the memory banks for something that would be useful. He didn't need passwords because he was able to read binary data and turn it into programs designed for the rover. He found the directory section of memory and started reading the file names out loud to the group in the room. When he reached the file for Herrenvolk, Max interrupted and said, "Check that file." A few minutes later Seymour responded, "I believe we have the group behind this. The file is an instruction book for those who believe they are the 'Master Race.' There are

Herrenvolk groups in every country and many places I have never encountered before. Min needs to record the list in her memory with the many groups identified. I am sending to her now." Seymour continued reciting the names of the files in the directory until he came across one called Medjay. Again Max interrupted and said, "Check that file." After a short pause Seymour came back with a verbal, "You did it again, Max, this is the file that connects the rovers with the military robots. It is quite large so I want Min to put it in her memory. I'm sending now."

Ruby could see the sweat running down Seymour's face. His teeth were clenched so hard his jaw was starting to swell. She firmly ordered the group, "OK. We need a break. Shut down for a while." She grabbed Seymour's hand and pulled the brain hat off his head. He was too weak to stop her. She ordered, "People in the room go get something to eat and rest up for a while. We will meet back here in two hours. Robyn, would you look after the children? Max and Min please find a way for my husband to look into the files Min has in her memory banks without wearing that

31

awful hat." Seymour took Ruby's hand and said, "We can't afford two hours. We must keep going." Ruby stared into Seymour's tired eyes and with her bright green eyes glaring and red hair swishing around her head emphatically declared, "Don't you get my Irish temper up. You will take a two hour rest or I will give you one by hitting you with this frying pan hat so hard you will be out for two hours!"

She held the hat by the handle and waved it in front of him and he knew, one way or the other, he was taking a break. Min then added, "I told Feeniks, and he said that's fine. He wanted to hide the rover in case the police robots came inspecting." That did it. Seymour went to lie down and take a short nap while everyone else did what they were told.

Ruby, however, went straight to the playroom. No one was in the room so she took a chair and sat next to the answer machine. She recalled what her husband had told her in bed one night about white moths being the spirit of someone that died. When Seymour later told her that Moses said, "Use my gift," she knew it was Glen's spirit in the moth. She sweetly whispered, "Hi Glen. I miss you. I don't know why you are here, but we need your help. Will you guide us like before? Tell us what to do. Please." Then Moses spoke without being rotated or shaken. Plain as day he softly said, "Dream." Ruby responded with, "Thank you, Glen. I love you." She hurried to tell Seymour but found him sound asleep in a lounge chair in their living room. She sat on the couch next to him and lovingly waited while watching him sleep.

An hour passed and Seymour opened his eyes to see the love of his life looking at him and smiling. When the fog left his mind, he softly said, "I've got to get back to work and find a way to decode that file  called 'Medjay.'" Ruby locked her eyes on his and said, "I had a talk with Moses. You were right, he is the spirit of Glen. He is here for a reason. I asked him to guide us. He said to dream." Seymour instantly sat up straight with eyes wide open. He almost shouted, "Ruby! I just had a crazy dream about Glen. I was back in the old lab, and Glen came in through his doggy door in the back. He pushed a water dish full of crystal-clear water over by me and barked at me. I had my hands cupped and filled with dirt. I dropped the dirt into the water and made it into a thick pile of mud. Then Glen went back to the dog door. He sat and stared at the door. When a big ugly rat came in with a green pine cone in its mouth, Glen grabbed and shook him until he dropped the pine cone. Then Glen took the pine cone and gave it to me to study. After careful inspection, I put it into the mucky water dish next to me. When I looked at the pine cone in the water it magically grew into a large and beautiful dandelion!"

Ruby thought to herself, "My husband has finally popped his cork! How can he get so excited about a crazy dream like that?" Seymour knew what she was thinking, so he said, "I will explain it all in the lab. I know what to do now. Thank you for being so smart and asking Glen what to do next. God bless Glen!"

Chapter 5
The Three-Step Plan

Everyone was back in the lab and focused on Seymour's excitement over his dream. He got everyone to sit down and told Min to pass on what he was going to say to Feeniks. Then he told them about the dream. Paul thought the tension made him snap and was suggesting a sedative, but Seymour just put up both hands and shouted, "Let me explain what it means!" Everyone sat down and gave him their full attention. He continued, "Every good programmer always gives himself a backdoor to get into the main program if something goes wrong. In my dream, the dog door is the backdoor for our enemy. Our back door was Glen's gift to me and allowed me to get into the main program through the antenna. The main program is where basic controls that power a machine on or off and motor commands are stored. The real powerful programs, however, are encrypted with a digital key that would take years to decode. That is why we cannot open the files we need to see. The water in the bowl represents all the powerful programs we cannot see because they are transparent without the encryption key that our enemy has. The dirt in my hands is our key that we will put on top of their key. This is known as a key-encryption-key, or KEK, and will make it impossible for them to see the programs. Now, it will take two keys to control or change the programs. The rat is the enemy, and he will come in through the back door to try and fix the problem. His first attempt would be to use his key to see if that fixes the problem. The pine cone is his key. Using Glens gift, I will get his key as soon as he tries to use it. After he leaves, frustrated, we will use both encryption codes to unlock the programs. The dandelion represents all the programs we will need to fight back. The

35

enemy will never get my key so they will be locked out forever."

No one ever saw a GA get excited before, but Max was swaying back and forth and declared, "It will work!" Min added that Feeniks agrees and is eager to get started. The people in the room were all smiling and discussing the plan. Ruby was just admiring her husband, thinking to herself, "How did he ever figure that out?" She got up, walked over to Seymour, put her arms

around him, pulled him close, and whispered into his ear, "How in the world did you ever interpret that dream?" He answered, "I didn't. You did." With a puzzled look on her face, she drew back and stared into his eyes. He continued, "When I woke up, I figured the dream was crazy and dismissed it instantly. Then you told me you had a talk with Glen through Moses, and he said 'dream'. That word triggered something in the gift from Glen inside me, and everything became clear. Like many faithful wives, you may never get the credit, but you did all the work!"

Paul apologetically interrupted, "Was there anything in the dream about the comavirus or a cure?" Min interjected, "Feeniks wants to know what he should do now." Others were waving their hands with questions so Seymour raised both hands in the air to get attention. The chatter subsided, and then he continued, "This is only step one of a three-step plan. We need to take control of the global network set up by the Herrenvolk groups. We can use their rovers and police to put everyone infected into hospitals, hotels, and other large buildings with beds. They will try and stop the robotic revolution, but we know who they are now, and if we get control, we can use their own network of police against them." The room was quiet now as Seymour further explained, "Step two will be bringing everyone out of suspended animation slowly or there will be worldwide confusion and mass hysteria." Paul interjected, "We must also eradicate the virus, or they will just slip back into a coma again." Seymour continued, "That is also part of step two. Then, step three is what to do with the people that created this mess. The final part of step three will be preventing Satan from getting this kind of control over others again. Right now, let's see if we can get through step one."

It was getting late, so people started leaving, and the GA group prepared to work through the night and have everything ready in the morning. When Ruby checked the children, she noticed that Devyn was sleeping on the floor at the foot of Stacey's bed. Bending over, she petted her gently and then picked her up and placed her on the bed at Stacey's feet. Ruby whispered, "Getting hard to make that jump, old gal?" Devyn softly purred her appreciation, flicked her tail once, and went back to sleep.

The next morning, the whole palace was as busy as a tribe of termites. People had found faith and something to believe in again. Seymour had formed a focus group for Phase 1 of the three-step plan and they were all gathered in the lab. Paul, Ester, and Jimmy were calling themselves the "Cure Hunters" and were on the far side of the lab gathering data to look for once the enemies programs were available. Robyn and Ruby were heading up a group to keep the people informed and all the children busy with home schooling. Stacey was in the garden helping with the planting and picking. She especially liked to make flower arrangements to place in the palace and brighten the rooms and hallways. The twins were in the playroom with Martin making something new out of E-Blox bricks. Like many twins, they enjoyed working together more than anything else. They would giggle and laugh as they decided the new project would burp or make a farting sound. Martin had exceptional electronic skills and added, "We can also make a beautiful glowing cloud around it." Devyn, however, never got out of bed and did not eat her breakfast.

Feeniks reported through telepathy to Min that he had moved the rover to a building far away during the night. He suggested that Seymour make a program that can copy the "pine cone" and store it in the rover's memory in a way that will keep the "rat" from knowing. After the "rat" leaves, we can try and retrieve the "pine cone." He used the code words just in case the enemy was listening somehow. He was moving into high-security mode because he knew the evil demons helping the enemy also had telepathic power. He did not think they could tap into his mental communications without his approval, but he was taking no chances. Feeniks concluded his telepathy to Min with, "After the 'water is muddy,' I will go home and wait for a 'telegram'." The new code word "telegram" told Seymour that he also needed to put a hidden program in the rover that would let Feeniks know the encryption code, "pine cone," had been stored in memory and the enemy, the rat, in the area had left. They did not know if any robot or person would actually come because all the rovers were linked by radio frequency transmissions through their antennas, but the GAs were now in high-security mode. It would be better to lose the rover than to lose Feeniks.

Seymour put on his brain hat, and through his link to Feeniks, mentally said, "Grab the antenna and hold on." A few short seconds later, he added, "OK, I'm in. Don't let go." Feeniks knew that it only took Seymour 8 minutes and 33 seconds to install the software, but to the people in the room waiting, it seemed like an hour. After removing the brain hat, Seymour told everyone, "All we can do now is wait and pray. Feeniks will let Min know if it looks like it is working as planned. I need a drink of something cold." Max held out a glass of cool water and said, "I anticipated that."

Meanwhile, back in the playroom, the twins and Martin heard Moses say, "Now!" His voice was stern and much louder than before. Andy questioned what it meant, and Joey replied, "Let's take a look at him. He might be in trouble!" Andy took the answer machine down from the shelf and placed it on floor. They sat in front of the machine and Joey held the base while Andy started to carefully remove the top to look into the room that housed Moses. Martin suggested, "Perhaps you should wait for..." – too late. Instantly the white moth flew straight to the door and out of the room. The twins both jumped back to watch it fly out the door and into the hall. They got up and went to look for it, but it was gone. Joey said, "Oh no!" and Andy added, "Now we did it!"

Although they expected punishment, they had integrity. Martin said, "I think you should go tell your dad." Andy mumbled, "Let's go tell mom. I don't want to tell dad." Joey agreed, and they slowly shuffled down the hall, side by side, with sorrowful looks on their faces to find their mother. Martin went to the lab to see how everyone was doing and prepare for a coming third degree on Moses.

Ruby was in the kitchen when suddenly something fluttered past her and went into Stacey's room. Immediately, her attention changed from planning dinner to investigating the thing that just flew through. When she entered the room, she noticed that Devyn was still on the bed in the same spot she had placed her the night before. There was a large white moth with wings spread out on the cats shoulder. It almost looked like the bug was whispering in Devyn's ear. Ruby slowly approached to get a better look. She could see that Devyn was not breathing, and the bug was a beautiful white moth. Suddenly, the moth flew up toward the sunlight coming through the window with a white fuzzy comet like tail following. The window was closed, but when it was just about to crash into the glass, the light got so bright Ruby had to close her eyes and turn her head away for a second. When she looked back, the moth was gone, the room was normal except for a sweet vanilla smell in the air. Her intuition told her that Glen had just taken Devyn to be with him in heaven. She knew now this was the real reason he had come. She whispered softly, "Thanks for coming early and helping us, too." She would have sworn in court that something just licked her face and said, "Your welcome." When she touched her cheek, it was wet! Then she heard the twins in the kitchen, "Mom! Mom!"

In the lab, everything went better than planned. Not only did Seymour get control of the rovers, but he also got control of the military robots. He had taken everything away from the enemy and was using this global power to protect all the people in the suspended animation coma. Feeniks was using this new global police force to monitor all the recorded Herrenvolk groups just in case they have space suits that protected them from the virus. Dr. Paul was now helping Seymour look through the programs that were transferred into the lab's computer to see if they could find a cure. Step one was done, and they were now working on step two. The adrenaline was high, and everyone was as busy as a woodpecker in a furniture factory.

The twins were back in the playroom joyfully working on their new project. Mom had told them they did the right thing, and Moses had a job to do. Having expected a punishment and getting praise was a big turnaround. Ruby was at peace in the kitchen planning dinner again. She knew the family would have to be told about Devyn and Moses. She was mentally preparing to make this news less shocking. Telling them all about Glen in the form of Moses would help. Telling them about the bright light being heaven would also help. Making the children milkshakes with a little extra vanilla for sweetness might also help. Somehow she knew everything was going to be all right. Most of all, she knew that in her final moments someone she loved would come and help her. This epiphany also instilled in her the belief that all of her family would not leave this world alone. She knew that a loved one would be there with each of them when their time came. She was so much at peace that she glowed. One might even say she had a halo.

Chapter 6
The Code

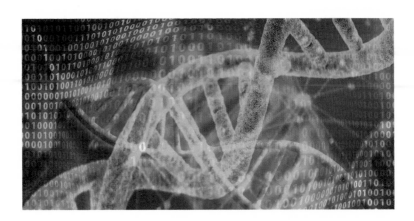

Dinner started out as usual with the family prayer by Seymour, but Ruby did not ask her usual question. Instead she told them that Devyn took a journey with Glen today. She filled in all the details and the original sadness turned to a melancholy mood around the table. Finally, she said, "Let's eat before it gets cold," and the sad supper began. Eventually, after a respectable pause from Ruby's announcement, Seymour took a sip from his shake. He wiped his mouth with his napkin and said calmly, "We made great progress in the lab today. All the rovers and global police robots are now working for us." He had wanted to be more robust in this announcement, but to show respect for Devyn, he restrained himself. Of course, Ruby knew how he felt, so she immediately added, "How wonderful! That's great news!" With even more enthusiasm, Jimmy added, "I have been working with Dr. Paul, and he is really smart! He thinks the cure for the DP20 is in the DNA of the comavirus itself." The twins wanted to get into the good news part of the discussion so Andy butted in with, "We are making a new machine!" Joey added, "Martin is helping, and he said he could make it fart, too!" At that, everyone had a good laugh. Laughter slowly subsided, and Stacey brought the family back to a somber mood by saying, "We need to have a little service for Devyn tomorrow. I would like to put her next to Glen on the farm in Indiana." Seymour sadly told her that was not possible right now. He also told her that she could keep Devyn's ashes in an urn and bring them to Indiana later. Everyone calmly agreed, and the dinner finished with quiet conversation.

On the morning of LD25, Stacey and her mom were at the kitchen table. They were discussing Devyn's service and making notes for the arrangements. Suddenly Stacey said, "I think I need to recite one of Papa's poems during the service, but it is a sad poem and really does not seem right." Ruby asked, "What's the poem about?" Stacey replied, "An old man that likes living in the dark because he lost the one he loved in daylight. I really did not pick it, Sally did. Last night, she kept flipping Papa's poem book open and pecking on that poem's title. Then she would bob her head up and down as if to say 'Yes! Yes!' I was just asking her what I should say at the service, and that was her answer. I tried to pick another poem, but she would not let me." Ruby took her daughter's left hand and gently held it between both of her hands as she responded, "One thing I've learned recently is to listen to the birds and bugs. You make the decision. I know whatever you do will be what Devyn wants." They finished making a chart of everything they would need for the service and then started spreading the word to be in the great hall at three in the afternoon if you wanted to attend.

In the lab, Paul and Seymour were looking at DP20 the comavirus that caused the coma under a microscope. It was sealed between two glass slides to prevent it from spreading. They both agreed it was fuzzy. It was like looking at it through some kind of a screen. Paul sadly proclaimed, "I've tried polarized light, infrared light, black light, bright light, different angles, and it's always fuzzy."

Jimmy was working on the lab computer. He was looking at all the notes and file names in the file directory from the rover. He had made a list of names and was checking them out with the universal language translator. He found one program named DCLXVI that translated into the Roman numeral for 666. DCLXVI has exactly one occurrence of all symbols whose value is less than 1,000 in decreasing order (D = 500, C = 100, L = 50, X = 10, V = 5, I = 1). Adding these up gives the number 666. Further investigating revealed this to be a satanic number so he brought all this information to his dad and asked if it might be important. Seymour complimented him with, "Great job Jimmy! Let me look at that program right now to see what it does." Decoding the software revealed it was a link to the gamma ray transmitters on the satellites that surrounded the earth.

When Paul heard this he got all excited and started looking for something that produced gamma rays. He gobbled down a cheese sandwich for lunch and went right back to bombarding the comavirus with gamma rays. He even tried radiating the comavirus for time periods related to the number 666. Results were less than disappointing, and Paul was getting frustrated. When Ester came up to him and told him it was time to go to the great hall for Devyn's service, he snapped back with, "She was just a cat! I don't have time for this!" Everyone would tell you that Ester could really control her body language. This was not one of those times. The look she gave Paul would have stopped a charging bull in its tracks. Paul picked up his notebook, put his head down, and headed for the great hall.

There was an elevated platform with a microphone stand at one end of the hall with folding chairs in front for everyone to sit. The room was very large, and the other end had tables with snacks and drinks ready for later. Paul sat with Ester in the last row because he wanted to look at his notes and did not want to be noticed. The normal crowd noise of people chatting did not bother Paul as he sat and reviewed his notes. Ruby tapped on the microphone, and the chatter slowly diminished into silence. She began with, "We are here to pay our respects to Devyn, our loving friend. If anyone has a story or wants to say a few words, please come up here now." One by one people went to the platform and described how Devyn had influenced them or just told pleasant anecdotes that sometimes made people laugh. Paul, however, was oblivious to the whole affair as he underlined passages in his notes and added notes for things he could try next. Stacey finally took her turn to speak. She went up to the microphone with Sally on her shoulder and said, "Sally wants me to recite a poem written by my grandfather. I don't know why, but she is insisting on this one. It's called 'A Door in the Dark.' So here it goes." Before she could start, Sally shouted, "Paul!" Now some people say she only shouted Caw, but if you were in the room, you would know it was a very loud "Paul!" Paul stopped writing and looked up at the platform. Sally was staring at him and shaking her head back and forth as if to say, "Stop what you are doing and listen." Paul closed his notebook as Stacey started:

"A Door in the Dark;"
"Back in the forest where the thicket can't grow
Where trees block the light from creatures below
Lives an old wrinkled man with a beard snowy white
Only he knows the reason he prefers constant night.

It is rumored he was cursed by a young witch
When he was in his youth and lived with the rich.
The curse, it is said, would cause him to die
If the light of the day should be seen by his eye.

46

If time could be turned to view the decades now past,
We would see that he lived on an estate very vast,
With servants and maidens too numerous to count.
Yes, he was heir to a fortune of the largest amount.

But his thoughts seldom ventured beyond his estate.
He was taught that the poor were just people to hate.
So he pushed whispers of conscience far to the side.
In his comfort and pleasure, he was content to abide.

Then the day came when fate would thrust open a door,
To a place the young man had not ventured before,
As a young girl with a face that glowed in the night
Seeking drink from a stream passed into his sight.

He was struck by her beauty that flowed from within
To the tips of her hair, to her eyes, and her skin.
He thought, 'This being of beauty so wild and free
Must be caught and be taught that she belongs to me.'

Tying his great stallion to an old tree by the brook,
He followed the girl through the hills to the nook
Where many fires burned to warm the beggars and poor,
A sight the young man had seen only one time before.

He remembered the raid he had made on this camp,
How they ran screaming into the night cold and damp
As his soldiers' horses trampled all in their path,
Driving these wretches from his land with great wrath.

He had just turned 16 at the time he recalled,
And his first smell of death left him slightly appalled.
But his father had praised him with shouts of great pride,
Giving him the black stallion and the sword by his side.

In the darkness he crouched and watched the young beauty,
Tending both needy and sick as though it were her duty,
While the firelight revealed as it caressed her face
She was a person of peace filled with heavenly grace.

He was thrown into remorse for his sins of the past.
As they dwelled in his mind, his soul grew more aghast.
Until there in the darkness, he conceived his great vow
To make this wondrous wench want to love him somehow.

There was an immediate change in his manner and way
As he gave food, meat, and coin to the poor the next day
Returning each night in the dark to hide by a tree,
Watching the young maiden his soul learned to be free.

47

The news of his great change soon spread through the land.
The poor came in great numbers to take gifts from his hand.
And he hoped and prayed she would come soon to his door,
Each night returning to watch her and yearn all the more.

His father grew dismayed by this new life of his son.
At the change of the moon, he decided what must be done
Gathering his army, they rode out one cold winter's day
To trample and kill every poor wretch in their way.

When the son finally woke and heard of this plan,
He raced through the hills and he thought as he ran
'Please God keep her safe!' but he found there instead
Her lifeless broken body amongst the numerous dead.

He carried her dead bloody corpse deep into the forest.
Where the sun cannot reach is where he laid her to rest,
For it was in the dark night all good he had learned.
Thus he stayed to live by her grave and never returned.

Back in the forest where the thicket can't grow,
Where trees block the light from creatures below,
Lives an old wrinkled man with a beard snowy white
Only he knows the reason he prefers constant night."

When she finished, Stacey just stood there for a minute with tears running down her face. She really did not want to recite this poem because it always made her cry. Sally never took her eyes off Paul. While Stacey cried, Sally stared at Paul and bobbed her head up and down as if to say, "Yes! Yes!" The hair on Paul's arm stood straight up and exposed the goose bumps underneath. Suddenly he knew what to do. He started to get up as he said to Ester, "I have to go to the lab." Ester grabbed his arm right above the elbow and pulled him back into the chair. Glaring into his eyes she growled, "Not now! Sit down!" Not wanting to invoke her ire again, he sat down. He could hardly wait for the service to end. He looked like a man with a red ant in his underpants. He kept fidgeting until Ruby finally announced, "There is food at the back if anyone is hungry." Paul turned to Ester and humbly asked, "Can I go *now*?" She nodded, and he jumped out of his chair and headed for the door. He almost ran out of the room. People just thought he was a senior on his way to the bathroom.

Paul's thoughts on his way back to the lab were mostly about Sally. He thought about what he would say if this idea worked and someone asked him how he knew what to do. He guessed he could always say, "A big white bird told me." When he reached the lab, he unplugged the microscope with the comavirus slide and took it into the storage room. He placed it on an empty shelf and let the plug hang down. He closed the door and turned off the light. It took about a minute for his eyes to adjust to the darkness. A small amount of light seemed to sneak under the door but not enough to matter. Feeling his way over to the shelf, he found the microscope, put on his glasses, and stared into the lenses. At first there was nothing. He waited. Eventually the fuzzy DNA started to come into focus. The fuzzy spots became very clear as the molecules of the comavirus faded into the background. There it was! A binary code chemically etched into the molecules. He verbally stored it into his tiny handheld recorder by saying, "00000110 space 00000110 space 00000110 triple space then repeat." He clicked the recorder off, fumbled his way to the door, and opened it. The room light was blinding for a few seconds, and then he saw Ester had come searching for him. She came over and took his hand and she asked, "Are you alright?" He responded, "Oh yes! Better than alright. I have a big piece of the puzzle. I just need to see how it all fits together." He went to a table and sat down.

Ester took a lab coat and, rolling it up to make a pillow, she said, "Put your head down on this for a few minutes. You need a short nap right

49

now." He knew she was right, so he wrapped his arms around the lab-coat pillow and instantly fell into a deep sleep.

Two hours later, Ester gently rubbed Paul's shoulder to wake him up. Max and Seymour were standing behind him. The microscope with the comavirus slide was in front of him. There was a small computer attached to the gamma ray gun aimed at the slide. Seymour said, "We built this from your notes and the recording that Ester gave us, but we wanted you to be the one to try it." Ester lovingly smiled at Paul as she told him to look in the microscope and they would start transmitting the binary gamma ray code. Still a little groggy, he wiped his eyes with the knuckles of his hands, put on his glasses, bent over the microscope, and said, "OK. I can see the fuzzy virus." Max flipped a switch and there was the low buzz that power supplies made when they were under a load. Ten seconds later, Paul sat back, took off his glasses, and said quite calmly, "We did it." He slid his chair out of the way and said, "Take a look." Max looked first and then Seymour followed by Ester. They all said, "There is nothing there?" Paul answered, "Yes! The DP20 comavirus destroyed itself when the code hit it!" They all laughed and gave each other high fives. "Victory!" was the celebration cry when their hands clapped.

Chapter 7
The Coma Ends

The news of the cure spread rapidly to all the people. Many wanted to know if they could go back to their homes on the outside. A meeting was called to tell everyone that it would still be awhile before the cave could be opened again. Some people were already packing up to go outside when Seymour called a meeting and announced, "It will take some time before we can open the cave. When we wake up the world, we do not know how they will react. We do have a large robotic police force to help control them and many delivery rovers to bring them food. Unfortunately, the crops are dormant in the fields and farmers need help getting the food distribution back to normal. Food may be a big problem. Please do not get too excited yet." Then Max addressed the people, "There are many other problems to be solved. I will be coming around to ask for your help. Think about what you could do." Even though his voice was identical to Seymour's, his robotic preciseness toned down the crowd's attitude.

On LD35, a new problem was revealed. The satellite program that emitted the coded gamma rays would wake up everyone at the same time. Special steps had to be taken to minimize panic. It took two weeks to get a few of the radio stations transmitting to the world the truth about the months they lost due to the coma. Portions of the global police were going to keep the Herrenvolk groups locked up and under close surveillance. The rovers were loaded with food and necessities to be sent to anyone that called for help. Feeniks was back at REED headquarters ready to get everyone informed and working again. On LD50, the time had come for the awakening. Seymour said a small prayer to the group, "God keep your people safe and protect us all from the evil one." He leaned over the keyboard in front of him and pressed the return key. The computer sent a command to the satellites and everyone held their breath. People everywhere started to wake up, and the comavirus was gone.

It took three days to turn the awakening chaos into regimented confusion. A week later, people outside of the cave turned on more radio stations. Cell phones on the outside were starting to come back. Radio stations were reporting mostly good news. There were a few reports of looters and thieves, but for the most part, the people were helping each other in a kind and loving manner. The leaders in the cave decided to open a small secret door to the outside world on LD65. A select group would spend a few days making sure it was safe, and then the people in the cave could return to their homes and use cell phones again. Everything seemed to be too good to be true. Ruby was worried.

The night before opening the secret door for the scouting group, Ruby said to Seymour, "I checked and there were no names of rich and powerful people in the Herrenvolk groups. There were no powerful politicians from any country listed in those groups. I know the Creature uses these people to do his evil work and make wars between countries. I know they are out there doing something sinister." Seymour trying to calm her replied, "That's why we are sending out the scouting group tomorrow. They will find out if it is safe."

The next morning before they could open up the cave, Feeniks sent a telepathic message to Min. He said, "Many ships surround island. Nothing electronic on them. Very hard to detect their purpose. Visual sighting only." Remembering

53

what Ruby said the night before and hearing Min relay the message made, Seymour say, "Wait! Don't open up the cave yet. Feeniks has detected a possible threat. A day or two more won't make much of a difference and it could save our scouting team." So with heavy hearts, the first scouting mission was cancelled. Feeniks sent people to high points on the island to use telescopes to investigate the ships.

Hours passed and finally, Min said Feeniks is reporting on the ships around the island. He says they are full of soldiers, but they have unusual battle equipment. First of all, there are no robot soldiers, everyone is human. Their weapons are ancient. The most sophisticated weapons are old laser guns with no computer-aided guidance. Communication between ships is with flags and blinking lights. Scouts also reported that they are using weapons that shoot projectiles with explosive powder. He believes they are called rifles. Then Min said, "Feeniks wants to know if anyone knows what is going on?"

Seymour told her to tell Feeniks, "It's the Creature. He's back. He lost our first encounter because of Glen's gift to me, and now he is making sure we cannot use that to fight him again." Feeniks recalled Seymour's telepathic memory of the trial and answered with, "Now I understand." Seymour was worried about the old fashion laser guns. They could be more powerful than computer-controlled laser weapons, especially in the hands of a skilled soldier. The Creature's first target was obviously REED because he wanted the island back. This was not at all what Seymour expected. He suddenly realized that the comavirus was just a distraction so we would not be able to see his real plan. A meeting was scheduled for all the leaders in the cave to discuss this new attack.

Everyone was working on something during the meeting of the leaders. Stacey was helping Ruby and Robyn make dinner. She would go into the garden with Sally and pick fresh vegetables for the salad. Sally always knew where the sweetest ones were as she helped in this task. Jimmy was with Dr. Paul and Ester plotting the DNA of the virus. They felt there was still a great deal to learn about the coma trigger and the self-destructive mechanism. Andy, Joey, and Martin were in the playroom working on their next invention. Martin had an innate understanding of physics and seemed to know how everything worked. Joey wanted to make the machine produce a really long farting sound. Andy wanted to use laser pointers and have beams of light shoot out whenever it made a sound. Martin got them to agree on LED beams that would break up into multicolored snowflakes when the machine farted or burped. He had an idea how to do this, and he loved a challenge. Max was in a different section of the lab working on a way to expand his force field to protect humans from bullets fired from old fashion rifles. Everyone was busy, even Martin's grandmother who was in the chapel praying.

It was taking days to decide on what must be done to protect REED headquarters. Feeniks had the people and robots to defend the island. He had mountaintop laser cannons that could set most of the ships on fire and sink them. They were put there when the Creature had control of the island. Many human lives would be lost, but they would be the creature's soldiers not REED people. Feeniks was not in favor of killing so many humans to save REED headquarters and asked for a better plan. Heated arguments were common and nothing was agreed upon. One night, Ruby took her husband's hand as they sat discussing the problem in their living room, and said, "Let the people decide. They are good people. Tell them everything, and let them offer suggestions. Who knows, maybe somebody's prayer will be answered." Seymour knew the wisdom in her words and hoped it would be his prayer that would get answered. He slept better that night than he had all week.

On LD77, the people were all asked to gather in the square in front of the palace at three in the afternoon. There was a platform in the middle of the square so anyone speaking could be seen and heard. Chairs and benches were set up all around the platform for people to sit. For some unknown reason to Martin, his grandmother made him come early and sit next to her in a chair near the front. The meeting started promptly at three. Seymour spent two hours explaining the Creature, the old war with the Creature, and the new attack by the Creature. He told them that Feeniks was against killing humans to hold the island. Then he asked for advice from the people. Opinions varied from "kill them all, they are working for Satan," to "forgive them all and let them have the island." It seemed like there would be no answer from this group. Martin's grandmother took Martin's hand, smiled, and said, "Go tell them what they need to hear." He said, "I'm just a child. They won't listen to me!" She answered, "You're much more than you know. Go tell them what they need to hear." Martin pleaded again, "I don't know what to say?" His grandmother answered, "You will know because it's in you. Just let it come out. Now go, child!"

Seymour noticed Martin making his way to speak, so he raised his hands and shouted, "Quiet please!" The arguing and loud discussions in the crowd dimmed and were gone when Martin reached the center of the platform. He felt a wave of confidence flow through his body. A strength that seemed to come from nowhere and everywhere. He stood tall, glanced at the entire crowd, and strongly proclaimed, "Fighting for peace is like shouting to cure deafness! You will only make others deaf, and you will only make others want to fight you." Seymour, Ruby, and everyone that heard his words suddenly woke up. They all realized they were in a coma all their life, and these words just woke them up. Martin continued, "Evil is not something you can put into a box and take into a room. What the Creature did is he took the love from the hearts of his soldiers and that made them appear to be evil. Our only weapon is to put that love back." He turned and walked back to his grandmother sitting in her chair covered with the blanket of pride and joy only grandmothers can receive. She thanked God for answering her prayer. Everyone that heard Martin's words woke up that day. Yes, this truly was the end of everyone's coma.

Martin's life also changed that day. He still tried to be a child and play with Andy and Joey in the playroom. People seemed to expect more from him now. Adults wanted his attention more than the children in the village. There was sadness in his eyes – the sadness we all seem to get the day we realize our childhood is gone. His grandmother, however, always brought him great comfort. Her love for him was now the greatest source of his peace.

Chapter 8
Step 3

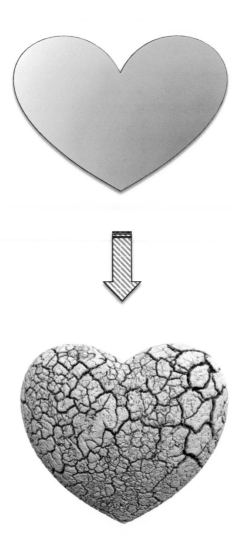

After the great awakening, everyone agreed that Feeniks should not let the Creature have the island. They should use the island and REED to perform occupational rehabilitation on the enemy soldiers. No one should be killed. A plan was forming, and it started with the "cure hunters," Paul, Ester, and Jimmy. They sent a memo to the planning group working on the final step of the three-step plan. It stated that a modified form of the comavirus could safely be used to put the enemy soldiers back into a sleeping state. They could then be stripped of their weapons and brought to the island. After waking, they could be shown how the Creature was sending them to their death just to further his cause. This must be done with love and without force or chains. They should start with one small ship and modify the procedure as they learn how to fill the enemy's hearts of stone with the warmth of love.

Max found a way to extend the force field around Feeniks to cover a small group of people and protect them from rifle bullets, arrows, spears, and other projectiles. The only downside was that it would not shield them from the laser guns. They needed something to stop the lasers, but nobody knew how. Paul and Ester decided to ask Martin because the last time they were stumped he had the answer. When they got to his house, Martin wasn't home but his grandmother invited them in for a cup of hot chocolate. She said she had just heated the water, and there was enough for all to have a cup. Paul did not want to stay, but one glance from Ester told him otherwise. The kitchen had a small table with four chairs and placemats on the table for each chair. The walls of the small cottage were filled with pictures of family and memories. There were a few awards that Martin

59

had received in science fairs in frames on the wall behind a shelf with trophies from sports. As they walked slowly to sit at the table, Ester said, "My name is Ester, and this is my husband Paul. We are working on trying to solve the problem you heard about a few days ago. Martin's talk inspired many to pursue a peaceful and loving solution to this situation." The old lady came out of the kitchen area with three cups on a tray. The cups were very old in design, and Ester was sure they added to the nostalgic ambiance of the room. The smell of hot chocolate covered with whipped cream made even Paul's mouth start to water. She placed a cup in front of Ester and replied sweetly, "I know who you are, dear. My name is Yolanda. I was named after my great grandmother." She then placed a cup in front of Paul and told him, "You need to loosen up, honey. Drink this and try and relax for a few minutes. I won't keep you long." Paul never realized how much his body language displayed the pressure he was under. Suddenly, her words brought a blanket of peace over his shoulders, and he sat back and tried to smile. Yolanda took her cup and sat facing Ester. She continued, "Now let's all take a little sip of this before we talk." Quietly, they all took a sip.

Leaning a little to her left side and with a little smile on her face, Yolanda fixed her eyes on Ester and said, "Girl, you got a big job coming. Putting love back into hearts of stone is not going to be easy. When you go back to that island and feel like you can't get it done, remember there are people here that love you and will help." Ester was surprised to hear that she was going back to REED. She had not discussed this or even thought about it until now. Yolanda smiled at her with that "I know something you don't" smile.

She continued to tell them how Satan had filled people with prejudice and hate. She talked about how Martin lost his parents to some of these people but eventually learned to fight the Creature and not seek revenge on the infected people. Paul had just taken his last sip of chocolate when Yolanda said, "Go now to the playroom. You will find Martin there with those two little rascals. Paul, I think you will find something they made very interesting." As they stood up, Ester started to pick up her cup and Yolanda added, "Leave the dishes, that's my job." She followed them to the door and smiled lovingly as they left.

On their way back to the palace, Paul turned to his wife and said, "I haven't felt this relaxed in weeks! What is it about that woman that puts me so at peace? She's better than any psychiatrist I've ever seen." Ester agreed and quickly changed the subject by asking, "Do you think I will need to go back to the island to help Feeniks?" Paul, not knowing what to say, just looked at her and said, "Maybe? I guess."

Arriving at the playroom, they heard Seymour telling a small crowd, "You are about to see the first demonstration of a machine invented by AJ and Martin called 'The Big Burp.'" In the middle of the room, elevated on a table, sat an E-Blox construction that looked like a person's face with a round hat on top. Seymour said, "OK boys, turn it on!" The twins just stood there with their arms folded across their chest and a scowl on both their faces. They wanted to call their invention the "Fantastic Fart Machine" but Martin

61

insisted ladies might be in the room and gave it the new name. Martin knew they would not cooperate, so he reached over and flipped a switch. Laser beams shot out in all directions for a few seconds from the round hat on top, and then the machine made a loud burp sound. Instantly the beams turned into a beautiful multicolored cloud.

Paul almost jumped over people as he made his way through the small group to get a closer look. When he got to the table, he noticed Seymour was standing there with wide eyes and his mouth open. He grabbed him by both arms and shouted, "I know! I know! It's exactly what we needed!" Turning back to the table, he noticed the cloud was gone and the beams from the laser pointers were back. Glancing at Martin, he said excitedly, "Make it do that again!" Joey butted in with, "You have to feed it." and Andy added "Just put one of those E-Blox bricks in its mouth." Paul quickly reached over, took a brick, and put it into the hole that looked like the machines mouth. A few seconds later, it happened again.

By the time the colorful cloud faded away and Paul turned around, Ester was standing directly in front of him. She took both of his hands and said softly, "I think you need another cup of that hot chocolate right now." Paul looked up and noticed everyone in the room staring at him. Only Seymour had a big smile on his face because he knew why Paul was so excited. The room was so quiet that Paul could hear his heart beating. Then Joey said, "I still think it should fart and not burp!" Laughter filled the room for a moment or two, and then things returned to normal.

Many questions came flowing out after that demonstration but all the people agreed to go home, organize their thoughts, and meet tomorrow. Then Martin could explain how the laser disrupter worked. Martin finally said to the crowd, "It was just an old science project I did a couple of years ago. It's really quite simple. I merely added a high-frequency light wave to modulate the sound wave of the burp that makes the photons in the laser beam lose phase relationship and disperse." Everyone said "Uh, huh?" and agreed to wait for the meeting in the morning with more of the technical people present. The people in the small crowd all headed for home.

On their way home, Paul mumbled to Ester, "I can't believe the biggest crisis in the world is being solved by children, birds, and grandma's." Ester's smile covered her face as she replied,

"Hey! Even Newton had to get hit in the head by an apple! Be grateful God is not throwing fruit at you." Paul smiled and made a profound statement, "Perhaps too much formal education can smother basic understanding and wisdom." Ester thought to herself, "Now there's some basic wisdom right there!" She lovingly took Paul's hand as they finished their journey home.

The morning meeting was very organized because the GA's spent the night setting up the agenda and groups. The basic outline of the plan showed how each ship could be put to sleep and the passengers could be safely removed. Feeniks would have to be in the extraction group to use his modified shield and keep the laser disrupter running. A comavirus ring around the island would put anyone trying to sneak in to sleep until the group could get to them. The virus-free waking buildings would have medical people and psychologists. Paul was convinced that the soldiers would be on some form of an addictive drug used to keep them doing what they were told. There would need to be a detoxification program in place. Paul, staring at a vase full of marijuana weeds given to him earlier by Stacey and Sally, said, "I think I know what will help in the detox." Everyone agreed the person to run all this had to be Ester because she was a medical doctor and a psychologist.

There was only one small detail where there was no agreement. The laser disrupter needed a song playing to keep it constantly working. They all agreed that it should be a song about love, but everyone had a different song. The song had to be their theme song. It had to convey what they were all about. Discussions were starting to get heated as they argued over why one song was better than another.

At noon, Robyn, Ruby, and Stacey entered with boxes of sandwiches and drinks. Stacey announced, "It's lunch time!" The bickering paused while the food and drink were being served. The room was fairly quiet when Stacey asked her brother, "What's the problem?" Jimmy replied, "They can't decide on the proper love song to be their theme song." Leaning over, she whispered to Jimmy something that no one else could hear. Jimmy nodded, put his sandwich down, and gathered his mother, Robyn, Stacey, and himself in the center of the room. He put his hands up and shouted, "We have arranged a little entertainment for you while you're eating." Robyn strummed a box to get the song started, and the quartet sang the song called Skidamarink.

{To hear song by quartet use camera and click QR code below. *Played with permission of PJM/Empower, P.O. Box 3, Flourtown PA 19031 and Peter Moses.*}

Skidamarink a dink a dink,
Skidamarink a doo.
I love you!

Skidamarink a dink a dink,
Skidamarink a doo.
I love you!

I love you in the morning,
And in the afternoon.
I love you in the evening,
And underneath the moon.

Oh skidamarink a dink a dink a dink,
Skidamarink a doo.
I love you!

The performance was followed by a very loud standing ovation. After lunch there were no more arguments about the theme song. The only comment made was that it was a silly song. Someone replied, "Perhaps that's what we need! The only way to fight a serious situation is with a little meaningful silliness." Everyone half-heartily agreed, and it was settled on.

Now the only problem was to get Ester and the other helpers to the island. They would also have to bring some medicine and equipment. Min finally said, "I will ask Feeniks. He may have a way." After a telepathic communication with Feeniks, Min informed the group that on LD90, the black-hole tunnel to the island would be open for one hour at noon. No one knew how Feeniks got this knowledge and no one asked. Trust ran high in the group and if Feeniks said it, they believed it. There were only a few days to get ready. They all started working on their task to make the plan work. It was like a beehive, where every bee knew it's job and did it.

On LD90, just as Feeniks had predicted, the tunnel to the black hole opened and a clattering of people pushed their equipment into and through the black hole to the island. On the other side, they emerged near the center of the island and made their way across the dried lake bed to REED headquarters. Feeniks had people waiting at the cave to help the small group of crusaders through the dry lake and up the bumpy paths. Many from the island were thrilled to see Ester, even though it seemed like they were just with her last week. Being asleep for two months helped as they all got acquainted and paired off to go to work. That night, sleep was difficult but the most tired managed to find their way into a deep slumber.

Ester was looking up at the stars from her sleeping chamber window and started thinking about Paul. At the same time, Paul was looking at the stars thinking about Ester. They were far apart, but they were also very close. Finally, Ester slipped into a deep sleep, but Paul had too many questions rolling through his mind. He laid in bed thinking, "How did Feeniks know when the tunnel would be open? Where did these Guardian Angels come from? Why do they have telepathic powers? How can an albino crow know so much? Talking moths? How can Seymour read and change software with his mind? Can the spirit of a dead dog come back in the form of a moth?"

Paul got up and made a cup of hot chocolate but it did not taste anything like Yolanda's chocolate. He never realized that love was the ingredient that made food taste better. He cleaned the cup and counter top, washed his hands, and went back to bed. It took a long time for Paul to finally find sleep. The questions would still be there in the morning so he put them out of his mind. He focused on stopping the Creature. The Creature must be stopped first. He wished Ester were with him. His last thoughts were about Ester when sleep finally came.

Chapter 9
Agape

The first month in the battle on the island proved that the Creature and Satan could be beaten. After the addictive drugs were removed from the enemy soldiers' bodies, over 90% were converted and turned. Some, however, did not want this change. Especially the higher-ranking people that did not want to give up being in command. Many of them were not even on drugs. Their addiction was the power they had over others. They were "power freaks." Ester knew they would have to be kept in an environment that prevented them from hurting others both physically and mentally. She also knew it would take longer to find a place for each of them in society.

In the palace, the leaders were preparing to send out the scouting party to the nearby town of Hidden Valley Village. LD120 was the day they would open a small door for six people to sneak out and investigate. Max would lead the group and protect them with his modified force field. They also had a small laser disrupter just in case. It played the same melody as the theme song, but the words were changed to appease people that thought "skidamarink" was a silly name. They replaced it with "Agape for you" and "Agape we do" throughout the song. Since Agape was the

Greek word for the highest form of love, it felt better. Another member said, "'Love for you, Love we do' is much better than that skida...whatever?" Feeniks told Min that he could feel the Creature trying to listen to their telepathic conversations. He was afraid he could not block them completely and suggested they do not use names of places or anything that could expose their location. He also told her the enemy

69

is using breathing masks and rubber gloves to get past the comavirus field that surrounded the island. Paul answered through Min and told him to make a spray of the virus. Make it similar to a misty cloud. It will go through clothing and contact to the skin will put them to sleep. She added, "Only a space suit could completely protect them from the spray."

Jimmy and Martin started meeting to discuss the possibility of making a device to detect a hating heart in a person. They asked the twins if they wanted to help, and Andy angrily answered, "Only if it can fart!" then Joey added, "And it will need to make a stink, too!" Martin replied, "We'll see what we can do," and he left with Jimmy to work on the project without the twins. Andy and Joey decided to make their own machine and make it the way they wanted. They went back to the playroom discussing how it should work. In their conversation you could hear, "It has to have a really long bathroom fart!" and "It has to smell like rotten eggs, too!"

After the passing of Devyn, Stacey and Sally grew very close. Stacey made a nest for Sally with an old basket filled with rags and paper. The nest was attached to the outside windowsill in Stacey's bedroom. The window was never closed so the bird could come in any time and be with her. Sally's crow's nest fit the purpose of the lookout platform of the same name on old sailing ships. Every evening before going to bed, Stacey would go over and pet Sally like she did with Devyn and say, "Good night." The bird did not seem to mind, as she would fluff up her feathers, settle into the nest, and be Stacey's lookout for the night.

LD120 came, and the door was opened. Max and five others carefully left the cave in a hidden area away from the path to the village. They made their way to the path, checking the sky for vultures and the surrounding area for snakes or any other rodent that might expose them to the Creature. Once on the path, they all stayed under Max's protective shield and made their way to Hidden Valley Village. The people of the village and surrounding farms had recovered from the virus coma and were almost back to normal. They had listened to the radio broadcast and understood what put them to sleep. The churches organized groups to restore order and help those that needed assistance. The mayor of the town, however, used the catastrophe to increase his police force and greatly increase taxes for the coming year. The little village was a perfect model of the problems the world now faced. Every country would have power freaks that desired power and wealth more than anything else. These people were Satan's easiest targets, so the Creature and his demons were busy using them to make divisions of hate in the world.

The mayor and his staff controlled all the radio, television, and newspapers. The only information the town people received from the local media was what the mayor wanted them to know. One person in the scouting group decided to put together enough money to buy the smaller newspaper that was on the verge of bankruptcy. He would move back into town, and with help from old friends, he would start getting all the news to the people in Hidden Valley. First they would change the name of the newspaper from "The Herald" to "Agape News." Then, they would get honest reporters and investigators to seek out the truth in every article. In a little while, they would have to set up radio and a television station that could get the public informed quickly on

71

serious events. All this would take time and many volunteers with the same loving mission. On LD125, Max and two other scouts returned to the cave. Three of the team stayed in town and started work on the purchase of the newspaper. The only real danger in the area seemed to be from the mayor and his very well paid police force, the Hidden Valley Police.

Paul missed Ester and could not talk to her since communications with the outside world were still shut down. He found himself visiting Yolanda frequently for a cup of her delicious hot chocolate and comforting conversation. In just a few short days, everyone noticed how Paul had changed. The nervous anxiety was gone and replaced with a new confidence and peacefulness. On the day Max came back, he asked Paul, "What happened?" Paul said, "What do you mean?" Max replied, "You're constantly smiling. You're not nervous all the time. Your demeanor is very different. What happened?" Paul smiled at Max and said, "Agape." There was a short pause while Max connected the answer with the question then he replied, "Wonderful."

Robyn, Ruby, Stacey, and Sally became a team known as "The Four Females." Over the months, they seemed to do everything together to keep the children's lives near normal in the cave. Families would often ask their advice on many subjects, including repairing an appliance to pet problems. The Four Females were able to give advice that helped because of the diversity of their group. In many cases, Sally would simply fly over to a spot and peck on something to show them where they needed to focus. It was a loving group that everyone trusted and wanted to be with.

Everywhere on earth, the Creature was being defeated. Everywhere, except in the political powers that ran countries with wealthy backers controlling them. The power freaks still had control over political organizations that ran countries. Satan worked hard to corrupt these leaders and make wars so humans could kill humans. Satan's master plan for worldwide genocide had failed, and he was back to his basic methods for destruction of the human race. REED had converted almost all the soldiers and sent them back to their homelands to spread love. All the ships around the island were gone. Not one human life was destroyed and this most of all angered the Creature, his demons, and their master Satan. Ester returned to the palace and was amazed at how Paul had changed. They spent more time together and many commented that they acted like newlyweds. The cave was totally opened, and the tri-blade helicopter and Mimi submarine were busy moving people to places when they were needed.

Ten months after the lockdown, on LD300, Stacey asked her mother, "I know I never knew Glen, but I was told that Devyn was his best friend. Can we take Devyn to the farm and put her next to Glen?" Ruby looked at her daughter and replied, "If tri-blade is not too busy, I suppose we could do that." Robyn was also in the room, anticipating the conversation, and commented, "He will be here in 30 minutes, and you can be back by suppertime." Knowing Robyn and trusting her words, Ruby's only comment was, "OK, Stacey get the urn and whatever else you think we may need." Robyn added, "Take Sally with you." Although Ruby thought that was a strange thing to say, she knew Robyn was aware of what would be needed so she answered, "OK."

The large door at the top of the cave opened and the tri-blade gently landed in a small field near the palace. Robyn had the passengers ready to board near the field so no time would be wasted. No one knew how to fly the helicopter, but that didn't matter because the tri-blade knew where it was going and how to get there. It was a two-hour flight, and on the way, Ruby told Stacey stories of past adventures with Glen and Devyn. Stacey had heard the stories before, but on this trip, they seemed to be special and more important. They landed in a field near the old farmhouse. When Stacey stepped down from the helicopter, Sally took off and flew out of sight. Ruby told her, "Don't worry, she will come back." The couple that bought the farm when Seymour's parents moved to the palace greeted them. The man said, "Hello, I'm Henry and this is my wife Daisy." Ruby was surprised to find that the couple were expecting them and had prepared a lunch for after the service. Henry said, "That phone in the house was quiet ever since the big sleep. Then this morning at around 6:00 a.m., it rang. And when I answered, I heard your voice say you would be out here before lunch to bury a cat next to the dog by the big old tree." Looking at Ruby he added, "It sure sounded like you. Was it someone else?" Ruby answered, "It was Robyn. We have similar voices." Then Stacey confirmed, "They sound the same."

Henry replied, "OK. Follow me." He took his wife's hand and led the small procession up a path behind the house to a large, old tree on a hill. Stacey carried the urn in one hand and held her mother's with the other. Under the tree was a small, flat marker in the ground with the words "Glen, My Best Friend," Placed in the ground next to Glen's marker was another newer stone with the words "Devyn, Glen's Best Friend." Below that, Henry had dug another small grave just big enough for the urn. Pointing at Devyn's stone, Ruby asked, "Where did that come from?" Henry replied, "I have no idea. It was just there when I got here so I knew where to dig." Stacey placed the urn in the little grave and stood up next to her mother with tears swelling in her eyes. Ruby took her hand, smiled gently at her, and turned to start a little prayer.

Before Ruby could speak, the flapping of wings got everyone's attention. Looking up, they saw Sally on a branch of the giant old tree. Next to her was a very black crow just a little bigger than Sally. Daisy pointed up at the two birds and said, "Look Henry! Sammy has found a girlfriend. And she's pretty, too." Ruby turned back to the little grave and said, "We are all gathered here to put these friends together in their earthly resting place. We know they are together in spirit now and enjoying God's heavenly peace. Amen." Everyone else added, "Amen." While they watched, Henry took a shovel that was leaning against the tree and started to cover the urn. He put some green sod over the grave to make it match glen's grave. During the final burial, Sally flew down and landed on Stacey's shoulder. She rubbed the top of her head on Stacey's neck right behind her ear and made a garbled crow call that sounded like, "Agape." She flew back to the branch, kissed Sammy, and the two birds flew off together.

During lunch, Daisy explained how Sammy started coming by the farmhouse and dancing on the front lawn until Henry threw some kernels of cow corn out to reward him. They named him Sammy after another black dancer that lived long ago. He started his dancing about two months ago and came at least twice a week. Stacey felt better knowing that Sally would be watched over by Daisy and Henry, but her heart was hurting from the loss of another friend. Ruby knew her little girl had just made the leap out of childhood.

Dancing Sammys

Chapter 10
Questions

After lunch, they went back to the helicopter to start the flight back home. Henry asked, "Are you a pilot?" and Ruby replied, "No. It is all automatic." Daisy then shook her head saying, "The things they can do these days." The couple backed up to get out of the wind as the tri-blade took off. On their way back to the farmhouse, Daisy commented, "Somehow I think there is more than just a dog and cat under that big old tree. I'm going to put some flowers up there tomorrow." Henry replied, "I've got to take care of the lower 40 tomorrow. We can get an early start."

On the flight back home, Ruby and Stacey had one of those Mother-Daughter talks that men could never comprehend. The words meant very little, but the transfer of emotions was enormous. Before they reached the cave, Stacey understood many things only women seem to be able to communicate to each other. Of course, there were many questions that never got answered, but she knew that was all part of being a woman. The last 20 minutes of the trip they sat in silence. Ruby was wondering how Robyn could know the future in such detail. She said to herself, "How did she get this ability? Where did she come from? How do all the dolphins, bugs, birds, cats, and dogs get involved in solving all these problems the Creature makes? How can a helicopter blade know what to do? How do those antigravity bricks work and where did they come from? Should I ask Robyn? Should I ask Max? And what's with this identical voice thing?" The mental questions ended when the helicopter landed in a field by the palace with Robyn waiting to welcome them back. The questions would have to wait because it was time to get Stacey to accept the loss of Sally and keep her busy making dinner.

Later that week, Andy and Joey wanted to demonstrate their latest invention. They were very proud of what they made without anyone's help. The playroom was small, so only a few people got an invitation to see the demonstration. They would show this great invention on Saturday at 3:00 p.m. Martin felt bad because he did not get invited, but Jimmy did. Yolanda told him to be humble and ask the twins if he could also come to the demonstration. Martin knew that his grandmother was very wise and went to the playroom to be humble. When Joey saw him enter the room he asked, "Martin, are you coming to the demonstration today?" Martin replied, "I did not get an invitation, is it all right if I come?" Andy said, "Don't be silly. You don't need any invitation. You're one of the master builders." Again the wisdom of his grandmother showed that humility could often bring praise. Martin smiled and replied, "Thank you."

Stacey made an announcement that the demonstration was about to begin, "Andy and Joey wanted me to recite an old limerick from our family that explains their invention." She then dramatically proclaimed,
> "A burp is but a breath of air
> That cometh from the heart.
> But when it takes the downward path,
> It becomes just a smelly fart."

79

Even those that had heard the limerick before could not help but laugh. Martin, however, did not laugh. There was something in that limerick that answered the main question in the project he was working on with Jimmy. He thought, "Now I know how Paul felt when he saw our first demonstration." Stacey concluded her introduction with, "And now here is the Fantastic Fart Machine." Joey reached over and pressed a button, and the machine lit up like a Christmas tree. A few seconds later, it made a loud burp. After another short pause, it made a very long bathroom-type fart. When the laughter stopped, Andy pressed another button on the machine and it said, "Phew!" Even Martin was laughing now, but he could hardly wait to tell Jimmy the answer to their biggest question.

Back in the lab, Martin turned to Jimmy and said, "James, what is the basic premise of our project?" Jimmy knew this was a serious question because Martin rarely called him James. "What do you mean?" he replied. Martin continued, "We are trying to make a device to determine if a person has a good heart, or a heart of stone. Right?" After a short pause, Jimmy answered, "Right." Martin went on, "Well, if a person decides to do good things for others in the world, it is the upward path. It is a breath of fresh air... the burp. But if a person decides to take a downward path and do bad things to others and the world then it is... the fart. It all depends on the decisions people make and those determine how his or her heart appears to others. People do not have a predetermined heart. They have free will and must decide on the path they will take. We cannot make a device that will decide what path a person will take. All we can do is show people what a good path is and what a bad path is. Like the machine, Andy and

Joey made and the limerick." Jimmy looked at Martin's smiling face and stared into his eyes. He replied, "Wow! I've heard that little poem many times and never got that message. What do you think it means?" It means we cannot make a device that will determine how a person will act in the future. That is the end of our project. That day, their project ended, but they would work together on new projects and a bond between Martin and Jimmy would soon develop.

The world was slowly changing, and people were choosing different paths for their lives. The LD calendar was dismissed, and the world was back on the same timetable. The people from the palace and mountaintop cave were relaxed. A small group, however, wanted some questions answered. They got together and made a list of questions. A meeting was called to discuss the list and hopefully get some answers. Present at the meeting were Seymour, Ruby, Paul, Ester, Robyn, Max, Min, and Feeniks. Seymour handed out the list and opened the meeting with a short prayer. "Creator of all, please guide us in truth and onto your path. Give us wisdom and understanding. Amen." The top questions on the list were;

1. What do the letters GA mean?

2. Where do you robots come from?

3. Why are you here?

4. Why do you have telepathic power?

5. Are there more GA robots in the world?

The rest of the list was about the tri-blade, anti-gravity bricks, black hole tunnels, Glen, Moses, the Creature, and the future. The GA robots in the room all scanned the list quickly and telepathically elected Robyn to speak for them.

81

She said, "I have been elected to try and answer your questions. We knew this day would come, and I will do my best to explain everything. You must be patient because, before I can answer your questions, you will need to understand the different forms of existence. I will start with your world because it might be easier to describe." Seymour reminisced about his days in school long ago. It felt like he was back in the lecture hall about to hear a dissertation on existence. Robyn moved to a position so all the humans could see her and started.

"More than 5,000 years ago, the Egyptian priests discovered a force we now know as electricity. Many of you understand this force today, and know it is due to the movement of what future investigators have called the electron. Everything that exists in your world has electrons and all the other electrons can feel the movement of one electron." To make it easier to understand, she offered an analogy. "Think of a beach and replace all the sand with marbles. If you reached down and pulled one marble out of the beach, all the close marbles would move to fill the hole. Then other marbles would move a little less to fill the space made by the movement of those marbles. This action would continue as the movement diminished the further away from the original hole you touched."

Robyn asked if they could all picture this in their mind. They all nodded and said, "Yes." She continued.

"Now imagine that each marble had a plan built into it that would allow it to configure itself into a blade of grass, or a fish if placed under water. Continue this process to imagine all the living things on earth and even the earth itself. Keep in mind that movement of one marble can still feel the movement of all the other marbles that exist in this chaotic universe of motion. Can you imagine an existence like this?"

Paul answered, "Yes, but what a mess of sensations and movements there would be." The others agreed with Paul and Robyn proceeded.

"This is what is known as the 'Physical

World' of existence. Even the light from stars very far away brings marbles to us and connects us to that star in this existence." Ruby starred at Robyn and said, "How beautiful!" All of the robots eyes turned a sky blue as they glanced back at Ruby. After all these years, Seymour suddenly realized this was the way they smiled at someone. So he looked at them and smiled back. Paul was anxious to hear more so he said eagerly, "Go on! Are there other existences or worlds of some kind?" Ester took his hand to get his attention and gently asked, "Do you need a cup of Yolanda's hot chocolate dear?" Paul got the message and replied, "I'm sorry. Please continue when you are ready."

Robyn continued.

"When you all said you could picture a beach made up of marbles in your mind, that picture had no marbles. That picture did exist in each of your minds, but it had no existence in the physical world. This type of existence is in what is called the 'Metaphysical World'. Dreams are part of this world. Thoughts and mental visions that exist in our minds, but do not exist in the physical world, belong to this meta-world. Universal concepts like infinity in mathematics come from this world. There are also beings that live in this world. Humans have given these beings names like spirits, angels, devils, and demons. What you call the Creature lives in this world. These beings do have existence but not in the physical world. Can you understand this explanation of existence?" Paul was getting nervous again. He had many questions, so he started with one of his biggest, "Do these beings travel from place to place?" All the robots eyes turned blue as they faced Paul, and Robyn answered, "There are no places in the meta-world. The only thing common to both of these worlds is time. They were there in the same past we were in. They are here in the same present we are in. They will be in the same future that we will be in. Everything else is separated by the Creator of these two worlds, but the meta-world is part of earth, too." Then Robyn scanned all the people with her sky blue eyes and stated emphatically, "Yes! Like Seymour said in his opening prayer, there is just one Creator of every form of existence."

Robyn patiently added, "There is still another form of existence that we are aware of but know less about. The Creator made this existence to reward all the beings that use the free will they are given to find their way back to live with the Creator. You often refer to this form of existence as Heaven. We also know this existence is real, but I am afraid we know very little about it. All we know is the Creator's plan is that we help everyone get there. We believe the Creator will personally greet us if we can get into this form of existence. Time, as we know it, is not present in this form of existence."

Seymour and Ruby held hands and smiled back at Robyn. Ester took Paul's hand and said, "What a wonderful explanation of everything." All the robots eyes returned to their normal colors as Robyn finished with, "All the questions on your list will be answered. It is getting late so think about what you just heard, and we will meet again later." The meeting ended and the robots all left the room. Ruby and Seymour just smiled at each other until Ruby finally said, "Let's go check on the children." Paul nervously blurted out, "But they did not answer any of our questions!" Then Seymour smiled at Paul and said, "I think they answered them all. They will give us the detailed answers soon." Ester added, "Let's go get a cup of that hot chocolate now." Then they all left the room.

All the questions were answered in great detail... But that's another story.

About the Author
Arthur F. Seymour

Entrepreneur, inventor, educator, poet, and philosopher:

Art studied electrical engineering at Christian Brothers University and earned his master's degree at IIT. During college, he authored one of the first patent applications on caller ID. He started his career at Motorola and was one of the first engineers to incorporate integrated circuits in color television. He later managed a group of engineers at Zenith Radio Corporation. Art launched E-Blox Inc. after 44 years of being the President of Elenco Electronics Inc. Presently, he has more than a dozen patents with a few still pending. Greek philosophy is still one of his passions.

Art and his wife, Maryann, were married on August 6, 1966 and have 11 grandchildren. They both took great joy in telling stories to their grandchildren at bedtime. Art claims these memories inspire all his books. His greatest inspiration in life, however, was his wife Maryann. Maryann went into the light while holding Art's hand on the morning of 9/11/2019. She was truly Art's Ruby.

Maryann, Art's Best Friend

QR Codes in this Book

There are **red** Links in this book that you can edit and be part of the Dynamic Editors List for SiBoRE™ books. Not all Internet sites submitted will be accepted. Internet Sites submitted must be judged as better than current Internet site and royalty free to use in a book. This process is believed to be unique and a patent has been applied for.

Note: An alternative to clicking a QR code is entry into any search engine the website shown when a camera is placed over the code block. You may also enter into any Internet search engine the site shown below for the QR code found on the page listed.

PAGE	SUBJECT	INTERNET SITE
Page i	Dynamic Editors	qr99.myeblox.com
Page 3	precognition	qr100.myeblox.com
Page 5	elderberries	qr101.myeblox.com
Page 22	plankton	qr102.myeblox.com
Page 24	Genocide	qr103.myeblox.com
Page 31	Master Race	qr104.myeblox.com
Page 33	Medjay	qr105.myeblox.com
Page 63	Newton	qr106.myeblox.com
Page 65	Skidamarink	qr107.myeblox.com
Page 65	Skidamarink Song*	qr108.myeblox.com
Page 69	Agape	qr109.myeblox.com
Page 83	Physical World	qr110.myeblox.com
Page 84	Metaphysical World	qr111.myeblox.com

* *Played with permission of PJM/Empower, P.O. Box 3, Flourtown PA 19031 and Peter Moses.*

This poem *Metamorphosis* describes how love can grow and change as it did in my marriage to Maryann.

Metamorphosis

Feelings aroused by youth in full blossom
Withstanding the test of loves first season
Brings forth a new joining into the kingdom,
And the bonding grows stronger without a reason.

A oneness that grows and thrives on the giving
Protected from harm by the armor of trust
Both laughter and tears stirred into the living
A soil created by mixing water with dust.

The purpose of joining three times fulfilled
As decades decay like ice without shade
Emotions evolving as each weakness is killed
Levels above for which they had prayed.

God's wisdom and patience was always a shroud.
This flickering flame has flourished and grown
Until it burned off lifes' obscuring cloud,
And the joy of real love was finally known.

The poem *Almighty Man* relates to the people in the story because all the characters had to make decisions that would affect their lives. Free will allows making these decisions even if the choices are bad or for the wrong reasons.

Almighty Man

Just who am I to have the power
To decide who lives or dies?
Be it for some noble cause
Or convenient alibis.

I've lived a life of variety
With countless changing scenes,
But never once did I behold
An end to justify this means.

I've let my want be the goal
Of so many of my choices.
I've closed my ears, so as not to hear
The need in other voices.

It will be said, by the living and dead,
His fate was his selection.
He knew the way and saw the truth,
But still did not seek perfection.

So here I stand, Almighty Man,
In all my majesty,
Only to know, how much I will glow,
Depends entirely on me.

The poem *Attitudes* describes how different characters in the story could look at the same situation and come to different conclusions.

Attitudes

Is it only frozen snow bringing cold and ice,
Or a kingdom that glistens with crystal?
Do you see the purple flower so soft and nice,
Or is your mind only on the thistle?

Do the birds in the trees make sounds that please,
Or a noise that distracts and offends you?
Does the smoke from leaves make you wheeze and sneeze,
Or does the aroma make old memories new?

When the climb to the top makes you want to drop,
Do you complain or enjoy the high scene?
Does the fireplace imply there will be wood to chop,
Or a colorful and warming machine?

When the rain comes down, do you sit with a frown,
Or picture the tulips to come?
Do you enjoy all the people who live in your town,
Or do you think they are snooty and dumb?

Does the moon in the sky bring a tear to your eye,
Or is it a light that keeps you awake?
And when leaves start to fall, do their colors enthrall,
Or can you only think of the rake?

When you see wild things, do you run for your gun,
Or stop and watch as they pass?
Do you enjoy hearing children play in the sun,
Or are they all just ruining your grass?

Is your neighbor a person that you must impress,
Or someone to call on in need?
Do you think only of buying a suit or new dress,
Or ponder the poor we must feed?

Do the aches in the morning seem like a warning,
Or a sign that you've seen a new day?
Do you find you are ornery and constantly scorning,
Or is life an exciting and wonderful play?

Is the way we believe then the way we perceive
What is good or bad in this world?
Or do we act naive as our own minds we deceive,
When our oyster is preciously pearled?

When that child inside first tells you "I'm Alive!"
What kind of future will you see?
For only you can decide, should this child survive,
The most beautiful being to be!

E-Blox Store

Get PowerFigure™ Characters from the story that light up!

Seymour E. Blox (known as Seymour)
Father in the Blox family who won the
first battle with the Creature. Use the
QR code on his back to see more.

Ruby
Mother in the Blox family who keeps
everyone on track and safe. Use the
QR code on her back to keep up to
date!

Robyn
One of the five Genetic Algorithm (GA)
robots. She can often see the future.
Use the QR code on her back and
keep up on her life!

Max
Another GA robot that can perform
technical jobs and much more. Use
his QR code to get news on exciting
new adventures!

Glen
The dog that does it all. The QR code
on him may just give you a surprise or
two. Check it out.

Devyn
The loving cat that protects the family
from the Creatures' spies. Check the
QR code on her for more information.

Get ready for the invasion of a whole new type of
LUMEN® PowerFigure™.
Characters from Story Blox™ come off the
pages! They come to life with our new line
LUMEN® PowerFigure™.

Also check out the invention from Andy & Joey.
(They wanted to call it Fart - Barf machine but Mom said no!)

Check store for availability.

Andy

Joey